GHOST RIDERS AT SHOTGUN BLUFFS

Zak Carter was a boy when the Ghost Riders arrived on the bluffs, shot down his parents and hustled him out at gunpoint. Now he's returned for his inheritance. Zak starts romancing the lovely Sarah Jo, who has also caught the eye of the renegade gang's sadistic leader. When she is kidnapped, Zak promptly straps on his gun and sets out to find her. Now he must break the outlaws' grip on the town . . . or die in the attempt.

Books by Robert Anderson
in the Linford Western Library:

GOLD FEVER
RENEGADE GOLD
THE GUN HAND
CONFEDERATE PAYDIRT

A	B	C	D	E	F	G	H
		83			13		

J	K	L	M	N	P	Q
	20					

LS 1636a

ROBERT ANDERSON

GHOST RIDERS AT SHOTGUN BLUFFS

Complete and Unabridged

LINFORD
Leicester

First published in Great Britain in 2011 by
Robert Hale Limited
London

First Linford Edition
published 2012
by arrangement with
Robert Hale Limited
London

British Library CIP Data

Anderson, Robert, *1945 Dec. 13* –
Ghost Riders at Shotgun Bluffs. - -
(Linford western library)
1. Western stories.
2. Large type books.
I. Title II. Series
823.9'2–dc23

ISBN 978–1–4448–1272–5

Published by
F. A. Thorpe (Publishing)
Anstey, Leicestershire

Set by Words & Graphics Ltd.
Anstey, Leicestershire
Printed and bound in Great Britain by
T. J. International Ltd., Padstow, Cornwall

This book is printed on acid-free paper

1

The Long Return

Zachariah Carter sat quietly in the saddle, staring moodily at the pitiful remains of the building, mute evidence of past habitation, while his mount dropped its muzzle and began to graze on the lush prairie grass.

The house had been burned down to its foundations years back, but Zak's nose twitched as though it could still sense the pungent odour of hot ash. His eyes traced the lines of walls, virtually invisible through the thick mesh of bush and weed that covered the site, then lifted to the stand of Nevada pine which lay behind. A powerful spasm of anger shook his tall, rangy frame, surprising him with its intensity after so long a time had passed. He'd buried his father deep under the shelter of the tall trees, but the cross he'd risked his life to plant had long since been removed.

'Damn them. Damn them all to hell,' he cursed aloud, raising his eyes to gaze at the nearby bluffs with a far off, flinty stare. Surely they could have left a man's marker to show he'd existed? It was little enough for anyone to ask of them.

He dropped his head, as though in prayer, then kicked his mount back into motion, heading for the old line hut that lay under the shadow of the bluffs. It had been the original ranch house when his parents had first taken over the ranch; only a tiny, one-roomed log cabin, but built strong and designed to be defended. An ideal first home for a time when ferocious bands of stray Indians still roamed the open plain, but it had long since been replaced by a comfortable new farmhouse close to the creek by the time he'd been born.

Zak had been reared as an only child, the three sisters that preceded him having died during, or immediately after, childbirth. Work on a small, struggling ranch had been hard, even for a young lad who knew no better. He'd helped out around the stock yards ever since he could remember, and by the time he was twelve he was a fully fledged cowhand, forking his pony out to the very limits of the spread to rein in the cattle, herding and branding as well as any of the itinerant cowboys his father sometimes employed for the round up. That was how Zak came to know his way up the bluffs, a secret he'd almost taken to the grave with him.

Shotgun Bluffs, a mighty baulk of rock that thrust far out into the plain from the larger cordillera that bounded its far edge, dominated the entire area. Its precipitous cliffs formed a natural boundary on one side of the ranch his parents had built up, and the waters that streamed down its towering crags supplied the creek that allowed them to water their cattle. There was a valley at its very centre, perched high on the slopes above the bluffs, accessed by a narrow winding canyon that was, so far as anyone knew, the only means of entry. Not that many of the local cowmen had ever bothered to brave its weathered, sun-blasted path. No point when even the valley was little more than a bare, rock-strewn mountain top.

Zak knew different, for he'd discovered the alternative path by accident while out chasing cows. He'd been rounding up a small herd of yearlings when he'd spotted the two mossy longhorns high above on the face of the bluffs, and immediately wheeled his mount around to hassle them down. The horse had more sense than the boy who rode him and refused to climb any further when the crumbling track narrowed to no more than a crack in the rock. The cattle were still above him, and Zak, with all the misplaced confidence of a twelve year old boy, promptly set out on foot to drive the beasts back down to the plain. Drawing closer, he drew out his handgun and

4

fired twice to scare the animals into retreat. The lumbering beasts gave him one baleful look and scampered off to even higher ground with an alacrity that defied their bulk. The lad, a set look on his face, headed determinedly after them.

It was a long, hard chase up the hill, but one which was rewarded in the end. The troublesome beasts succumbed to his persistence, and were at last dispatched back towards the plain, while he continued to climb the vestigial traces of a route that led ever upward. At long last, after traversing an almost vertical wall of rock, the slopes grew less precipitous and he entered the mouth of a canyon, the source of a spectacular series of waterfalls that eventually formed their own creek. The canyon widened into a hanging valley, with its own deep waterhole, fed by water running over the cliffs from above. He walked on, and the vegetation, at first sparse, gradually began to appear more verdant and lush, but the deep valley he finally clambered into took him by surprise.

Although the local ranchers had told the family that such a valley existed, this green and fruitful oasis in the midst of the barren, rocky slopes took him by surprise. A babbling brook led from the still, clear waters of a wide lake at its very centre to supply the canyon's rock-bound waterholes. There was grass, lush, green and sweet, and cattle too, perhaps a dozen head that he could see. God alone knew how they'd made it that far! The track Zak had followed led up cliffs and rock faces, steep enough to be called vertical in places, and not even the sure footed, wild and mossy longhorn cows could have negotiated those.

He knew all about the trail that led up to the plateau of course. Everyone around knew of it by reputation, though few, if any, of their neighbours could have described it from personal experience. He also knew the entrance lay around the far side of the bluffs from their ranch, a good half day's ride. It would take him a week to negotiate the way on foot, and he'd never be able to drive the cattle before him. Shrugging his shoulders he retraced his steps down the mountainous slopes, arriving home late enough to face the wrath of a father terrified he'd lost his only son.

The Ghost Riders arrived later that same year, riding up through the bluffs like the wraiths they were named for, and taking the lost valley for their own. They weren't really ghosts of course, merely a gang of rough and ruthless outlaws seeking an easily defended hide out. People in the local town nick-named them the Ghosts of Shotgun Bluffs because, it was alleged, they vanished into the hills, only emerging to raid and rob before they melted back into their rocky fastness. That wasn't true either, though it would have taken a brave townsman to come out and say so openly, for the so called Ghosts used the town's facilities as often as any of the scattered ranchers and their hands.

They had been led by an ex-confederate colonel, Hugh Prescott, a man who, at the end of the War between the States, refused to accept that the South could be defeated. Under his rigid leadership his command had continued to fight Union forces from swamps and forests right across the South, fading away whenever the fighting got too hot and emerging to start again in another state. Gradually, over the years their tactics changed and they began to hit civilian targets, ostensibly to provide the means for the struggle to continue, though by now most of the patriotism had gone and the proceeds were unashamedly shovelled into their own pockets. Eventually, with his command attracting the wrong kind of recruit, Prescott sank to armed robbery, pure and simple. Military discipline might have gone, but the Colonel, as he still termed himself, was a big man with a mighty temper, well used to keeping order by the sheer power of his will and, where necessary, with unremitting ferocity and cruelty.

Aaron Hallevisz was one of these new recruits. He'd risen high in the ranks of the outlaw gang to take over the post of the Colonel's chief lieutenant, largely due to his icy ruthlessness and the quicksilver speed of his draw. Nicknamed 'Preacher' from his predilection to dressing all in black, down to the long tailed frock coat he would wear all year round, his background was as a tough NCO in the army of a tiny central European Dukedom. Having killed his man in a drunken quarrel, he'd escaped his homeland en route to the Americas one step ahead of the executioner, and swiftly gained a reputation as a fast and ruthless gun in the Western plains of his adopted land. And when the Colonel finally died, it was he who took over and led them on the most virulent raids on towns and railroads within striking distance, though always far enough away that their own hideout remained a secret from any federal posse brave enough to chase them.

Despite the outlaws' rough and ready ways, some good did accrue to the town from their custom. The fruits of their wicked ways pumped money into the town's economy; saloons and the general store did particularly good business. The old adage of not messing in your own back yard rang true too. The town's bank and other local businesses seemed to be immune from the outlaws' piratical raids. There were of course, more fights, gunplay and even murders, often disguised under the name of self defence. More girls in the saloons too, much to the disgust of the God-fearing folk of what had once been a very quiet back water.

For a year or two the ranchers clustered around the bluffs had been left alone too, but that wasn't destined to last for much longer. A little rustling was only to be expected from a hungry bunch of outlaws, and that was the way it started, but all too soon it was ending in tragedy. Just what happened to initiate the move to clear out the area immediately adjacent to the bluffs no one ever knew for sure, but as soon as it was authorized by the Preacher, the intimidation began.

Zak's own parents, with their ranch nestled under the bluffs, but furthest from the canyon-like entrance, were largely immune from the outlaws' incursions at first, while one after another the neighbouring ranchers were forced out of their holdings. Some left of their own accord after a so-called friendly visit from the gang in which the Preacher was always a notable member. Others stayed to fight and were cut down mercilessly; ambushed or burned out, even goaded into drawing on the Preacher himself. Despite all the evidence piled up against him, his cold-eyed killing was always excused by witnesses as self defence, for no one was willing to cross the fearsome lieutenant of the Ghost Riders.

The war finally reached the Carter Ranch one dark, autumn night and Zak began to muse on it while his horse trotted on towards the old line hut. His pa's sensitive ears had caught the sounds of stock disturbed and he'd gone out in his long johns, shotgun in hand, determined to deal with a blatant attempt to rustle so close to the house. He should have known better. The warnings had already been issued and he was shot down in his own doorway. The Preacher himself had been there, Zak saw him with his own eyes, but there were enough witnesses brought forward later to swear he'd been drinking in the town's principal saloon at the time.

'Start packing,' his ma told him, her tears still fresh on her worry-lined face, and stark fear in her eyes for the son who looked so much like his father.

'No.' Zak, at fourteen years old, was enough of a man to know what was due to his sire. 'We have to bury him.'

'Do it then.' Ma had seen that same stubborn look on her husband's face, notably when she'd tried to persuade him not to interfere that very night. 'We'll say a prayer over his remains before we leave.'

The young lad had speedily done as he was bid, sorrowfully burying his father deep in the sandy ground beneath the pines, and wasting valuable time in whittling a cross with his father's name carved on it. By the time he returned to the house his mother had two cart horses coupled to their old buckboard and a growing pile of belongings heaped on its bed.

'I'll help, Ma,' he'd offered, but she'd taken his hand and pointed towards a nearby rise where four riders sat motionless in the colourless light of dawn.

'No more, it's all over,' she'd told him.

'But Pa . . . '

'Your pa would understand,' she'd interrupted him wearily and climbed up on to the wagon, her tears for the man and his ranch vying with the fright in her eyes.

Zak had stared back at the riders, black hatred in his heart, but utterly impotent to do anything while they spurred their mounts forward. He didn't even have a gun to hand, something he'd afterwards suspected his mother of ensuring. Would he have used such a weapon to defend his home? He liked to think so, but he also remembered the bitter taste of fear that fought with the hate, and the knowledge he could still have been in his bed when they lit the kindling. The entire Morrison family had died in just such a way no more than a couple of weeks previous. A tragic accident the sheriff had called it, glancing nervously over his shoulder at the dark clad rider who'd called in to offer his condolences for the poor occupants.

'We should have said words over his grave, Ma,' he'd told her mournfully while he looked his last on the house, watching the conflagration consume his erstwhile home while its flames vied with the rising light of morning.

It was the last time he ever spoke of his father to her.

2

Shotgun

There was no one left in town to remember why it had been christened Shotgun. Had it been named for the bluffs? They were less than a day's hard ride away. Or had the bluffs been named for the town? Chicken or egg? And why Shotgun? Only the founding fathers knew the answer to those questions, and they were long since gone, moved on or dead, most likely both.

Whatever the answers, the town became home to Mrs Carter and her young son, Zachariah, following their enforced evacuation. Ma hadn't even bothered to involve the sheriff in their troubles. She had no faith in that gentleman meting out justice, not when so many others had died before. He was a good enough man, as all the town knew, but quite incapable of standing up to the hardcase outlaws that rode in from the bluffs. Not that he didn't have a hint of steel in him, at the very least he'd taken on the sheriff's role and tried to keep the peace in town, which was more than any other of the town's folk. The truth was that the entire population were in the Ghost Riders' pocket, and with a host of outlaws ready to back the Preacher's gun play, it was likely to remain that way forever.

Not that its newest inhabitants overtly showed any intention of over-setting the balance either. Zak's mother took on a job helping out in a rooming house. Mrs McGonagle was growing old and found herself happy to have someone as young and strong as Mrs Carter to take the heavy burden of responsibility from her shoulders. Zak meanwhile, found himself a place in the livery. He knew horses and he was used to the hard, physical labour and long hours. Mr Hardie was his employer, a considerate man who eventually became more of a friend than a boss to the young lad.

Young Zak already knew how to shoot, both with the rifle and the handgun, but with whatever spare time he could find he began to polish his skills. He concealed his abiding hatred for the men who'd killed his pa behind a façade of cheerful affability, but a secret thirst for revenge had lodged deep in his heart. Sooner or later he'd take his chance, and either shoot the Preacher down, or die in the attempt.

Apart from his boss at the livery stable, he made only one other close friend in town. Despite his air of apparent cordiality, there was a darker side stamped into his nature by the tragic death of his father, one that could prove disturbing to the unwary, and it kept others at a distance. Not that he was ever known to lose his temper, but the manner in which he kept his feelings under such cold control was in itself an unnerving experience.

The one true friend he did make was Sarah Jo. Two years his junior and bright as a button, she often went riding from the livery where she had her very own pony stabled. He most often acted as her groom on these expeditions and the two of them would happily ride off for hours at a time, under no instructions other than to stay away from the bluffs. She, too, didn't play with the other kids. Her father, Mr Mountjoy, was the bank manager and he considered her station put her too far above the other children in town for friendship. He made Zak an exception to the rule, for Sarah Jo's consequence as his daughter, demanded that a groom should ride with her wherever she went. And he never thought for a moment that his own self-important stance would lead to her making the lad a bosom friend rather than the humble servant her father deemed him.

Sarah Jo loved to gallop and so did Zak, allowing her to take the risks none of her other escorts ever dared. She liked to watch him practice with the gun too, tossing battered cans into the air for him to shoot down, or lining them up in rows while he fanned his pistol to pepper them back down. And at length they'd end up at an isolated stretch of the creek where they'd cool themselves down, shucking off their clothes to splash contentedly in the cool waters of the stream while he taught her to swim.

A year into their brief companion-ship, and aware of his eyes on her burgeoning curves, she'd taken to wearing her underclothes into the water. Not that he ever thought of imitating her modesty at that age, leaving Sarah Jo to save her maidenly blushes by turning her head aside while he stripped.

Of course she didn't peep at him! What sort of a girl would do a thing like that? Until eventually, at long last, he too covered up and began to lead their expeditions away from any such temp-tation, all too aware of her charms and

19

her susceptibilities. Zackariah Carter was fast falling in love with the banker's pretty young daughter, despite understanding the inevitable opposition that any suit he put forward would face from her father.

In the end it didn't matter. Disaster struck just when it seemed as though life was beginning to go right for the Carters. Mrs McGonagle decided to sell up and allowed his mother to buy into the rooming house at a very fair price, and Mr Hardie was beginning to talk about taking Zak into partnership at the livery. Not that they were given any time to celebrate . . .

He was just seventeen when his mother died, cut down in the cross-fire between a gang of thugs led by the Preacher and a couple of tough cowboys, drifters who were passing through on their way to another job. For once things hadn't gone entirely the outlaws' way; the cowboys packed guns, and they knew how to use them. The fight started in the saloon, but soon spread out into the street where Mrs Carter was caught out in the open. A stray shot, or so they told him, but to Zak's knowledge, none of the Preacher's shots ever went astray. Useless to tell him it might have been the cowboys who shot her and that if so, she'd already been avenged by their own deaths, for he knew in his heart the Preacher was guilty as sin.

He shed hot tears over her body at the undertakers, then, with ice cold hatred pumping through his veins, strode off to find his own gun, eventually running the gang to earth when they rode out of town. The man he regarded as his own personal nemesis, the Preacher, was at their head. He took careful aim and fired. There was time for one shot only before he melted into the cover of a back alley, and he missed his intended target. Another of the outlaws had veered across his path at the last moment and took the bullet meant for his leader. Not a bad wound, but one that would demand revenge. An eye for an eye, swore the Preacher, and began to scour the streets for the man who'd dared to stand up to him.

Zak, in the meantime, was preparing for his mother's funeral. Despite its immediacy, most of the townsfolk attended, but it was only afterwards, sobbing in his room, that Zak received any true comfort. Sarah Jo tracked him down and sat on his bed holding him, cradling his face against her bosom while she stroked his hair and softly crooned into his ear.

He could never tell afterwards just when the sorrow in his heart began to melt under her tender ministrations. He only knew that all of a sudden he was aware of her soft breasts brushing his cheeks, of her long legs hot against his own. And then she was trembling in his arms while he rained kisses on her face, her lips, her throat, and most exciting of all, she was kissing him back, matching his most fervent caresses with those of her own.

He checked then, all too aware of where their red hot passion would lead them. He wanted her then and there, wanted to enjoy her soft body, flushed and excited on the bed with him while they consummated their love. But she was still his youthful friend, still the innocent young girl who trusted him. He couldn't bring himself to snatch the comfort she was all too ready to offer, not when the shadow of the Preacher lay between them. Even then he knew that sometime or another he'd have to shoot it out with the feared outlaw or flee and, to the girl's dismay, he walked out on her.

He didn't know where to turn. Tom Hardie, who might have counselled him otherwise, was nowhere to be found and he wandered into one of the saloons in a daze. Mrs Carter had been a devout worshipper at the local church, and had brought her son up to follow the ways of the Lord. He'd never taken hard liquor before, but he needed the courage alcohol could instil, and it wasn't long before his words began to slur. He slammed his money down on the bar and ordered another whiskey.

Jennie was one of the prettiest whores working in the saloon, and certainly one of the youngest. Neither was she averse to the glint of coins laying in plain view on the counter. She knew Zak by sight too; knew he was the handsome young lad from the livery stable, though she'd never spoken to him before. Well, that could easily be set right by a girl as experienced as she.

Zak's eyes opened wide when she settled herself at the bar by his elbow, the warmth of her body pressed deliberately hard up against his own. Young as she was, she'd already learned the tricks that turned a man on.

'Will you buy me a drink as well? Please?' she'd wheedled. Then steered him to a remote table when he ordered the entire bottle. This was one mark she didn't intend to lose.

She was good company too, had to

be, her job depended on it. She drew him out, and for the first and last time in his life he began to make empty boasts: about how he'd already shot down one of the outlaws; and how he'd take the Preacher, face him down man to man. Jennie already knew that one of the outlaws had been wounded, but when Zak disclosed he'd been the one to do the deed and was brave enough to boast of taking on the redoubtable Preacher next, it made her look at him in a new light.

Here was no half drunk boy, but a real man. A living, breathing hero, and she straight away invited him to her room. He staggered to his feet and would have fallen heavily if Jennie hadn't put her shoulder under his arm. She'd had plenty of experience of drunks in her young life, and leading him upstairs, though not as easy as she'd envisioned, didn't overtax her strength.

Once there she let him loll limply on the bed and stepped back to survey him. The intimacy of his new surroundings brought Zak back to full consciousness immediately. The bedroom smells, cheap perfume and even cheaper sex struck hard in his nostrils, and he was in the act of rising to leave when Jennie unhooked her dress. He paused on the instant, swallowing hard, while its neckline drooped and she worked on the next fastening. A girl in Jennie's position always had a certain amount of cleavage on view, but as the fastenings gave one by one, the slopes of her pale breasts were laid enticingly bare, and inevitably his body began to react to their subtle charms. All of a sudden, the bodice dropped and he became aware of just how little the girl wore beneath it. Her plump breasts swayed invitingly, youthfully uptilted, the saucy pink nipples stiff beneath his ardent stare.

Jennie grinned cheekily and thrust down her skirts and petticoats together, unabashed by her nudity while she posed in indecent deshabillé for his benefit. She'd already calculated the extent of his innocence and knew she'd have to make the running in his seduction, no hardship to the girl when he was such a clean cut, handsome young lad. He'd make a nice change from most of her clients, ugly customers like as not, more than ready to cuff her if she didn't cater to their whims, however perverse. Many of them too, were happy enough to simply throw her roughly on to the bed with her skirts thrust rudely over her belly while they took her brutally with no other thought than their own enjoyment.

'Your turn now, honey,' she told him huskily and began to unbutton his shirt, gurgling softly when his greedy hands began to explore her lush, freshly bared body.

★　★　★

Next morning Zak awoke in a sorry state. His head hurt abominably, his limbs ached and, worst of all, his mouth

27

was furred with a vile tasting coating he longed to swill away with a draught of sweet, fresh water.

He opened his eyes and stirred; attempted to sit up and wished he hadn't. The room swayed crazily about him and he sank back with his eyes closed. He'd seen enough! There was a girl lying dormant on the bed beside him. She had no clothes on, and although sleep had softened her features, leaving an impression of youthful innocence, the events of the night flooded through his consciousness with painful clarity. He groaned when the memories struck him and forced himself to sit up again, throwing his legs over the side of the bed before he could fall back. What was her name? She had told him, though it was by no means a formal introduction in the circumstances! Jennie, wasn't it? That was it, Jennie.

He staggered across to the window and, throwing it open, breathed in great gulps of fresh air. It may have served to clear his head a little, but he didn't feel any better for it. He shouldn't have been drinking, shouldn't have laid with the girl. He had man's work to do! He dressed quickly, ignoring the nauseous swirl in his head, threw a couple of dollars on the dressing table and left. He needn't have paid; Jennie may have been young, but some things are learned quickly, and she'd already rifled his purse for as much as she dared.

The cold light of day, early as it was, brought new fears to the lad. With his head still reeling and the hot mists of his immediate anger rolling back, standing alone against the Preacher with his formidable record as a gunfighter didn't seem such a good idea. Nevertheless, his desire for revenge hadn't weakened, and he thrust back his shoulders and checked over his pistol.

That was when Tom Hardie found him.

'Get out of town right now, boy.' The advice was good and Tom backed it up

29

with a mount already saddled and laden with all the lad would need to make good his escape. Provisions, a hurriedly packed carpet bag, a rifle, even some money, as much as the liveryman could afford.

'I — '

'Don't be a fool, Zak. The whole gang's in town, with the Preacher himself at its head. They know it was you who shot their man down. Everyone in town has heard how you admitted it in the saloon. The Preacher's in a stone cold fury, the more so since you aimed for him and threatened to face him down. Go then, ride out now. Keep riding until you find a part of the country where they've never even heard of the Ghost Riders.'

'Damn the Preacher. It's him who killed Ma and Pa. I've got to take him before I die. I — '

'He won't face you on his own.' Tom interrupted his young friend's explanations with a ruthless assessment of the facts. 'He'll have men ready, willing and able to back him up. There's no revenge to be taken against such odds. You'll only get yourself killed too.'

Zak hardly seemed to hear his mentor and friend. He was staring up at the apartment above the bank and a pale face framed in a window. He could see the accusation in her tear-laden eyes and abruptly he mounted, wheeled the animal around and dug in his heels.

3

Growing Up

The young lad rode his horse hard throughout that long, fateful day, never allowing his guard to drop, and only stopping to snatch a few hours of restless sleep when it became too dark to pick his way forward. In truth, he was driven more by the ghosts of his own conduct than any real fear that the Ghost Riders would run him down. The knowledge that the Preacher would demand revenge on the person who'd dared to fight back may have spurred him on, but the resilience of youth soon learns to cast aside fears which are no longer imminent. In fact, it was the sick discovery that he'd loved and lost that troubled him the most. Sarah Jo would never look him in the eye again, let alone snuggle into his comforting arms.

The night he'd spent with Jennie had been fun; the memories of her nubile body arose unbidden while he lay in his lonely blankets under the starry sky. He'd enjoyed romping with her, though he burned with righteous wrath against himself when he admitted it. He should have remained true to the memory of Sarah Jo and his mother's strictures. Eventually he fell into a fitful sleep vowing never to cross the threshold of a saloon again.

Next morning he woke with the dawn feeling more refreshed. The Ghost Riders hadn't caught up with him, and if they'd ever bothered to take up the chase, his hard riding must have left them trailing helplessly in his wake. Native caution still prompted him to check his backtrail on a regular basis, but with the sunshine warm on his back and riding at a more measured pace, the optimism of youth soon began to bubble to the fore.

He had a living to make, and the whole world to make it from. Why, he could do anything, and when he camped that night by a tumbling stream in a mountain pass, he met another young lad eager to make his fortune. They formulated the idea together while they sat around the campfire yarning; they'd volunteer to ride with the Pony Express, no longer a mail service, but the security arm of the redoubtable Pinkerton Agency.

Since Zak had ridden from a very young age and knew how to handle a gun, he found the arduous life of a Pony Express operative easy to adjust to. The service was tough, and his employers pulled no punches, but a life of constant danger and exercise swiftly turned him from a boy into a tough and confident young man. He spent two years in the saddle in all weathers, over the most punishing of terrain, never knowing when a band of Indians might take a liking to his scalp, or an outlaw to his bulging saddle-bags. Or he'd be guarding a stagecoach or bullion wagon, with all the weight of its safety in his hands, or joining a posse to track down the worst and most violent of badmen. It was thirsty work, more often than not, lonely too, and it wasn't long before his resolution to avoid a visit to the saloon deserted him.

It was no sort of job for anyone who wanted to make his fortune either, he decided eventually, ruefully counting out the small store of coins remaining in his pocket one boozy evening, and promptly signed on for a trail drive.

Pushing cows on the well worn trails to the railheads wasn't any easier or better paid, but he was less likely to get shot at by bloodthirsty outlaws. There was still the occasional badman to fight, rustlers and stray bands of renegade Indians mostly, but it was the sheer unremitting grind of rounding up the obstinate steers that led to the frequent accidents that cut short many a cowman's life.

Zak settled into the routine of the job quickly. He was a grown man, able to act on his own initiative and take charge when times got tough. Soon he was promoted, ramrodding the roughest, toughest, meanest bands of cowboys, driving them down the trails as ruthlessly as they drove the cattle in their charge. And if they turned on him, he'd face them down with fists or guns, until the day his fearsome reputation for scrupulous honesty secured him the job of deputy to the sheriff of Wishbone County.

Wishbone County had been a God-fearing little township, not unlike his own home town under the bluffs, until the Jones boys moved in. The sheriff was no mere cipher like his namesake in Shotgun, however, and with his deputy sworn in, he began to engage in the thankless, and very often dangerous task of cleaning up a nest of vipers stiff with wrongdoers.

Vince Jones was the eldest of the three brothers and Elroy the youngest, but it was Nathan that was the driving force behind their worst atrocities. His predilection for brutal intimidation, backed by a fearsome reputation for gunplay, had won the brothers leadership of a band of swaggering bullies, and they intended to hold the town for their own discordant ends.

For his part, the sheriff formed a posse to face them down once and for all, throwing his forces against them in a vicious fire fight through the streets of Wishbone County's principal town. For once, good seemed to have triumphed over evil when the gunslicks were driven clear out of the territory by the vengeful posse. Vince and Elroy Jones were dead meat; shot down, like so many others of their gang, on the streets where they were cornered. The remnants of the shattered band scattered to the four winds, those still left living riding out at the gallop in fear of their lives.

Nathan was made of sterner stuff, or maybe he just lived to seek revenge on his brothers' killers. The sheriff came on him outside the livery stable and went down in a hail of bullets, his gun barely clearing his holster before the ruthless gunman cut him down. Another and another died before his blazing pistol and the surviving members of the posse dispersed, their gains blown out of the water by a single fearsome gunslick.

Nathan Jones turned his talents to seek out the last of the lawmen, challenging Zak to meet him gun to gun in the street at noon. The former deputy, by now wearing the sheriff's badge himself, waited patiently in the saloon until the appointed hour, steadying his nerves with a final drink. He was used to using a gun to defend himself, and had often defied other men who set out to kill him. He'd even stood face to face out on the streets before, with nothing but the speed of his draw standing between him and oblivion. But he'd never faced down a gunman with such a fearsome reputation as Nathan's. A reputation that had stood the test too; the sheriff had been a rough, tough lawman, but he'd gone down beneath the outlaw's guns, so too the other members of the posse unlucky enough to meet the vengeful badman.

The waiting stretched Zak's nerves, and screwing his courage to the sticking point was never so hard. The townsfolk depended on him, he told himself, depended on his crumbling resolution. If Nathan Jones emerged from the fight victorious then a fresh reign of terror would engulf the citizens of Wishbone County, and the best of them would have died for nothing.

Jennie was a distant memory of a faraway place, but there were other Jennies in Wishbone, and he wished he could seek the same comfort in their arms as he'd found in hers. It was nearly time and, eschewing their undoubted attractions, he checked his weapon again and again, working the pistol's movement with professional thoroughness and gauging how easily it slid from its freshly oiled holster, before striding towards the door.

The sidewalk was empty, his footsteps echoing eerily on the wooden boards in the unaccustomed silence, until he stepped into the street and surveyed its dusty length. Nathan Jones detached himself from a shady nook further off and lounged into view, striding deliberately on a course to interrupt the steady walk of the new sheriff.

Zak Carter felt as if he were in a dream, his movement mechanical, and he wondered if his opponent's mouth was as dry as his own. Was he frightened? He was certainly apprehensive about the part he had to play, but he'd been through too much to run scared. He'd been sworn in as sheriff, and the future of Wishbone County depended on him. Depended on the speed of his draw.

He saw the moment begin in Nathan's eyes, the glint that told him the other was going for his gun. It was a moment that seemed to go on forever; he was reacting, but the action seemed to develop in slow motion. His gun was in his hand and the focus blurred, the movements suddenly all too quick. He fired, and fired again, but the second shot hadn't been necessary and the citizens of Wishbone County were drifting back on to the streets, staring down at the body of the man who'd held them in thrall. Nathan Jones was dead, shot down by a faster gun, and the townsfolk stared at the cold-eyed sheriff with a wary fascination.

He learned then that the ice cold control that made him such a dangerous opponent when pitched against gun-toting renegades, dealt him no lasting favours. The townsfolk were grateful for his help, but they were frightened of the hard man with the gun who'd freed them from their oppressors. The mayor did his best to reward the new sheriff's bravery, heaping honours on the young man and offering him a job for life, but Zak had seen the sidelong glances and knew he'd never be truly accepted in Wishbone.

He was weary of the struggle and he

wanted to go home. The mayor protested, but without any real conviction, and like most of the other townsfolk, he was all too happy to see their flint-eyed sheriff ride out now the job was done.

As for Zak, he was ready at last to take up his birthright. The birthright his parents had bought with their blood, their sweat and their tears. He owned a ranch, their ranch, far away under the bluffs of a far off territory. He hadn't seen it in over five years and, for perhaps the first time, he acknowledged it. He was going home, and all the Ghost Riders in the world wouldn't stop him. He wasn't aiming to force a fight on the Preacher or his gang of desperadoes, but the ranch belonged to Zachariah Carter, and he was all too prepared to defend it if anyone sought to take it away from him.

It wasn't that easy, of course. Wishbone County to Shotgun Bluffs was a long journey for anyone to accomplish — several months — and he had to stay alive in the meantime.

4

A Man Back Home

Zak took his time to stake out the old line hut before he approached too close. It still stood four square and could have harboured an enemy, might even have been regularly used by the Ghost Riders. On the other hand, they hadn't torched it, so might not even been aware of its existence.

His every instinct told him the building was unoccupied, had never been occupied, not since he'd left the ranch so many years before. Still he made his approach with the same care that had kept him alive for the past five or six years. At the last he took it at a run, gun in hand, and kicked in the door with a crash that shook the whole structure to its foundations. There was nobody in residence and he felt foolish enough to chuckle at his fears.

The construction was more than a simple line hut, as he very well knew. The erection of an easily defendable headquarters had been one of their priorities when his parents first moved west. The building backed up against the precipitous cliffs under an overhang, with narrow windows covering the open approaches, and consisted of a thick sod roof over solid timber walls. Not a comfortable house like the one he'd grown up in, but a fortress in miniature, complete with its own water supply fed off the bluffs above.

Zak's horse came first in his priorities, and he set it loose in the old corral after carefully inspecting the state of its timbers. It was in a better state of repair than he had any right to expect, even down to the old, tin-lined trough which he conscientiously filled from the stream utilizing an ancient and battered leather bucket that dripped half its contents on every trip. If that was to be the extent of his troubles, then he'd be a happy man.

The house, too, was in good order. The birds had evidently found for themselves they were able to slip through the gaps between the dried and cracked leather curtains that was all that covered the slit windows, but the door had remained solid enough to stop the depredations of larger animals. Until he'd arrived, that is, for the ancient leather hinges had collapsed beneath the weight of his unconventional entrance. No matter, a few hours' hard labour would see everything shipshape, and he'd never been shy of work.

Evening came quickly, but for all of that, he'd completed his immediate chores, and in the last fading moments of the twilight he stared up at the bluffs above. Were the Ghost Riders still living in the depths of the hanging valleys above? Or had they too found their time, and moved on?

He didn't know the answers to those

questions and told himself he didn't care. He'd returned to take up his inheritance, not seek revenge on killers who, for all he knew, had already met their just deserts. He'd spent years fighting back the guilt for running from his parents' killers, but those years had also brought him some measure of wisdom, enough to understand what would have happened if he'd stayed. The kid he'd been would have gone down fighting tooth and claw, but he'd have been just as dead as his mother and father, and his tormentors just as triumphant.

He was back now, back on the ranch that had been his parents', and was now, by rights, his own. If he had to fight, then by God he would, but he wouldn't blindly seek his enemies out. If the Ghost Riders still lived on Shotgun Bluffs, as the very emptiness of the range under its shadow suggested they did, then setting up his camp at the very foot of the bluffs would sooner or later bring down a pack of killers upon him. But they would have to make the first move.

If the Preacher was riding proudly at their head, then he would take his revenge for the deaths of his parents as well as his inheritance. Unlike his late father, who'd been an essentially peace-loving man, all too willing to see the slightest sign of good in others, Zak had learned his lessons the hard way since leaving Shotgun. His reliance lay on the gun in his hand, for he understood from his own experiences just what sort of welcome to expect from the Ghost Riders if they found him unprepared. Nor would he expose himself against the light in the way his father had, or wait for his opponents to fire the first shot. Any outlaw foolish enough to cross his path would swiftly be shown the error of his ways.

It was a determination that Zak had learned from years of living rough.

★　★　★

The town of Shotgun hadn't changed much over the years. Zak sat his horse at the edge of town and surveyed its main street in the still light of early morning. He'd ridden in for provisions, enough to withstand a prolonged siege if necessary, and consequently had set off early. The far off canyon that led to the top of the bluffs may have been a hard day's ride from the town, but his own, more humble, abode was only a couple of hours' distant across the gently rolling prairie.

He allowed his horse its head and began to amble slowly down the street. Business was beginning to open up; the blacksmith was labouring at his forge already, and across the street one of the shopkeepers was up a rickety ladder making running repairs to his sign. The livery was straight ahead, but no longer bearing the name of Hardie, and across the way lay the bank, starkly uncompromising in its solid construction, just as he'd always remembered it. No doubt Sarah Jo had been married years since.

Zak dismounted outside the livery stable and led his animal into its murky depths.

'Take care of my mount,' he ordered a scruffy urchin, the very image of himself so many years before, who seemed to be in charge. 'Saw the name on the board outside. What happened to Mr Hardie?'

'He's long gone, sir.' The scrawny youth returned the answer respectfully. He had a good job and intended to keep it, and that included being polite to customers, even if they did ask the silliest questions. Why, everyone in the county knew old Mr Hardie had been shot down by the Preacher when he refused to tell the outlaw where his protégé was.

'Gone?'

'Dead, sir. He's got a stone in the cemetery.'

Zak stared into the distance as though his eyes could pierce the buildings that hid the site of the old graveyard from him.

'That's right, sir. Up on the hill, past the church.'

'Thank you,' Zak returned his appreciation gravely and tossed the lad a dime. 'Does the bank still belong to Mr Mountjoy?' Now, why the devil had he asked that question? It was none of his business who ran the bank. He didn't need a loan, or at least, not just yet.

'Yes, sir. He hosted a party a couple of weeks back, roasted a couple of longhorns and invited the whole town to join him.'

'Doesn't sound like the man I used to know,' Zak grumbled.

'Mr Mountjoy wanted the whole town to welcome his daughter back home. She was packed off east to study at some sort of fancy academy years back. Don't know why, less he wants her to teach school now she's back. She's much too old for learning, and much too pretty. Never seen such swell gowns as she wears.'

'Sarah Jo?' It wasn't really a question, more a murmur of a half remembered playmate's name.

'That's her name, sir. Do you know her?' The boy looked at him with new respect. The stranger's trail-scarred work clothes might not pass muster, but he was evidently well connected.

'Once upon a time,' Zak admitted, 'but I doubt if she'd recognize me these days.' Or even want to, he decided, though he kept that lowering thought to himself. He knew he'd betrayed her more than his parents when he ran off.

'If you're talking about me, then you're wrong. I do recognize you, Mr Carter.' The lady's voice was familiar, though its inflexion held a more mature and cultured tone than the one he remembered. 'What are you doing here in town?'

Zak stared at the office door, or rather at the woman framed in its opening. Sarah Jo had grown up and he barely managed to control the urge to whistle before he touched the brim of his hat.

'Just picking up some supplies,

ma'am. Moved on to my father's ranch a day or two back.'

'Get my mare out for me, Mike.' Sarah Jo watched patiently while the stable lad jumped to do her bidding, leaving room for Zak to study her figure.

She'd always been on the tall side for a woman, and that fact hadn't changed none. Must have got it from her ma's side of the family; Mr Mountjoy was short and fat. Her face had filled out and taken on the beauty it had always threatened, with her eyes still as luminously bright as he ever remembered. Her body had filled out too, taking on curves he could only have imagined all those years ago, all too obviously an eminently desirable woman despite the spartan lines of the riding dress she'd affected.

'Are you staring at me, Zak?' Once the stablehand was out of earshot, Sarah Jo turned her attention on her old friend, using his given name for the first time. One eyebrow cocked in question.

'You're a mighty fine looking woman, Sarah Jo,' Zak temporized. 'Man could be forgiven for staring.'

'Some men's eyes rove more than others, Zak.' Sarah Jo's face held the faintest hint of a frown, and he knew she was accusing him. It wasn't just his own dreams that had been shattered when he left town so abruptly, and the expression on her face told him everything. She'd been in love with him that night, just as he'd been with her. Useless now to plead how he'd left her for the sake of that very love, not when he'd headed straight to the bed of a pretty whore. That was a story she evidently knew all about too. Every gossip in town would have seen to that.

'I left town a long time ago.' It was no answer and Zak knew it. Knew too that Sarah Jo was still the girl in his heart, still the woman he wanted to hold. Only now she was farther from his reach than ever.

'I still remember that night, Zak. The Preacher will too!' Sarah Jo was serious now. 'He might not recognize you straight off, but someone will. The Ghost Riders have eyes in town, more than you'd credit. When he learns you're back to haunt him, he'll come calling. And he won't come alone.'

'I'll be waiting.' There was a steely glint in the cowboy's glance that Sarah Jo didn't remember in the boy she'd played with, the boy she'd once loved. An icy determination such as she'd seldom seen marked in other faces, and never thought to detect in the gentle light of his. The cold, hard stare of a man who could kill without a qualm.

'Then you're a fool, Zak Carter. The Ghost Riders are too powerful for you, no one man can go up against them on his own.' She turned when the sound of a horse being led up interrupted them, and flashed the stable lad a smile of gratitude. 'Thank you, Mike. Hold her steady while I mount, if you please.'

The briefest flurry of petticoats frothed around Sarah Jo's ankles while she leapt lightly into the side saddle, then leaned forward to address Zak again.

'Leave town while you still can,' she advised, schooling her face into an expression of haughty indifference. 'Leave the territory altogether, Zak. There's nothing for you hereabouts; not your parent's ranch, nor me. Not while the Ghost Riders are in charge.'

Zak stared dumbly after her when she left. What had she meant by that speech? Not while the Ghost Riders are in charge, she'd said. Did that mean she might change her mind if they weren't? Did it have to mean anything? Just because she'd shown some concern for his situation, it didn't give him any right to assume she still thought kindly of him. Did she?

'Anything else, sir?'

Zak grinned at the lad's unfailing politeness and ruffled his hair.

'Guess that'll be all for now,' he decided.

5

A Warning from The Preacher

It was late afternoon before Zak saw Sarah Jo again. After purchasing his provisions, he'd retired to the saloon where he'd sat morosely at a table near the bar, alone with a bottle of rye. Jennie no longer plied her trade at that establishment, but one of the other whores had taken her lead and promptly been rebuffed. He didn't want for company, not with the ghosts of his parents and old Tom Hardie vying for his attention. Nor did he want comfort. His thoughts were much too bleak to contemplate the delights of a warm and willing body.

Thus it wasn't until the bottle was finished that he strode up the hill towards the cemetery. He should have been falling down drunk, but his tall,

rangy, straight-held form didn't stagger, not even sway, while he made his way to his mother's grave at the back of the plot, where he held a lonely vigil over the simple wooden cross he'd planted with his own hands. He stayed for perhaps a half hour, clasping his hands together in front of his chest and praying as he'd never prayed since he'd last seen her alive.

Mr Hardie's resting place was harder to find. He hadn't been there to pay his respects when his mentor died, and he was sorry for it, sorry the man had died at all. Hadn't expected the stone either. Tom Hardie had been a prominent and popular citizen in town and his friends and colleagues had defied the Ghost Riders to raise a proper monument to the man they all revered. All Zak knew was that his friend was dead.

'He died for you, Zak.'

The meaning of her words didn't sink in for a moment. Zak had been aware of someone approaching; had recognized her scent from their earlier meeting, but not acknowledged her presence until now.

'What do you mean?' A half formed suspicion began to unfold and harden in his mind. He'd lit out fast all those years before, but he'd never been aware of any attempt to chase him down. There had to be a reason the Ghost Riders hadn't followed him.

'He sent the Preacher off in the wrong direction. I watched while a gang of them interrogated him only a couple of minutes after you left town. They galloped off towards the old railhead; reckon they thought you'd flee east. Or more likely that was the story he fed them.'

'What happened?'

'They came back again later that same evening. Useless to follow you by that time, you'd be too far off to even think of taking up the chase, but they still had revenge on their minds. Nobody saw them do the deed, or if they did, they were smart enough to keep quiet. Tom Hardie was cornered in his own livery and dragged down a dark alleyway, where they beat him to death.'

'How do you know what happened?'

'There were no witnesses to connect the Ghost Riders with his murder, but plenty of people heard his cries.' Sarah Jo choked back a sob. 'I did myself, though I didn't know who it was at the time.'

'No one came to his rescue?'

'The town was running scared of the Preacher and his men, still is. You, of all people, should know that.'

'I shouldn't have run off,' admitted Zak. 'I wouldn't have if I'd known they'd blame Tom.'

'It was the only sane thing you did that day,' she returned promptly and a little tartly. 'If you'd stayed the Preacher would have come for you and Tom Hardie would have died anyhow. He was the sort of man you could rely on, one who'd never have left you to face a pack of gunmen alone.' She hung her head, and if he'd looked, he would have seen the pale bloom flushing into her cheeks. 'I was angry with you, but I was glad you'd escaped.'

'You knew what I'd done, who I'd been with,' collaborated Zak. 'I saw your face in the window accusing me. I could see the tears running down your cheeks, eyes red with crying. I might not have run if I hadn't seen you; hadn't seen what I'd done to you.'

'My father told me what happened at the saloon. He never approved of our relationship and he knew the way I looked up to you, even accused me of . . . ' She blushed fierily. 'Well, it doesn't matter what he thought we were up to on that day, or any other, come to that.' She stared directly into his eyes, asking the question that still hung between them. 'Why did you do it? Why did you choose her?'

'I was drunk.' Hell, that was no answer, but it was the only one he could give. He couldn't tell her he'd been scared stiff, ready to take his comfort where he could find it. Not when she'd offered him her own body that very same afternoon.

He knew she'd read his mind by the way she raised her head so proudly. He'd turned down the chance to make love to her, for a roll with a cheap strumpet in the nearest saloon. Had his motives really been so pure as he liked to remember? Or had he realized what an encumbrance she'd be if he had to flee? Hell, when he had to flee!

'You still are drunk,' she told him, her eyes flashing contempt while her nose wrinkled at the stench of sour whiskey. She was angry and he half expected her to slap him and stalk off.

★ ★ ★

Any reply he might have made was stillborn when the Preacher lounged out of a nearby back alley and signalled to his men. Three of them spilled out of the church's rear entrance and stationed themselves to cut off any retreat in that direction, while a couple more ranged themselves directly to the

Preacher's rear, ostentatiously showing off the rifles in their hands.

Zak silently cursed himself for forgetting where he was; he'd allowed himself to grow careless while he'd taken what comfort he could from Sarah Jo's company. They'd never have crept up on him unawares otherwise. His brain spun faster, calculating the alternatives.

What would the outlaw do? What could they do? The Ghost Riders usually committed their murderous deeds where there was no one to bear witness, or, at best, made their killings look like self defence. Did they plan to murder Sarah Jo too? Or would the Preacher insult her, tempting him to draw?

Surprisingly, or at least so to Zak Carter, Sarah Jo herself was the first to break the deadlock.

'Good evening, Mr Hallevisz,' she began, her voice as composed and welcoming as though the murderous gang had showed up for a prayer meeting. 'Have you come to escort me home?' She stared up at the sky where the sun was beginning to set. 'There was no need, you know. Mr Carter was about to accompany me.' She slipped an arm through his and turned him towards the church, then to Zak's surprise, took the Preacher's arm too.

'The sunset is a much paler spectacle back east,' she tilted her head archly, and looked straight up at the outlaw's face. 'Don't you find it so, Mr Hallevisz?'

'I never had much time for sunsets when I lived east of the Mississippi, Sarah, but you must have noticed how your face lights up my heart whenever I see you. Why don't you call me Aaron?'

The guttural accents of eastern Europe grated in Zak's head. What the devil was Sarah Jo playing at? Come to that, what was the Preacher playing at? Flowery compliments had never been his trademark, not when there was a man to kill less than three feet away.

'What would my father think if he

heard me calling a man by his given name?'

Zak stared at the way Sarah Jo was playing with the killer. She may as well have batted her eyelashes at him!

'Perhaps he'd think you cared for him,' the outlaw replied easily, 'as he cares for you.'

Sarah Jo's lips curved into the sweetest of smiles, leaving Zak's free hand to ball into a fist, and he'd have flung the punch if the Preacher's men hadn't fallen in behind them.

'Are you playing with me, Mr Hallevisz?' she replied flirtatiously. Then, following the slightest of pauses, 'Aaron.' A merry laugh, and she skipped towards the heavy wooden door that guarded the apartment above the bank, drawing both her companions in her wake.

There she offered her hand for the Preacher to kiss, which he did with surprising grace, and turned to Zak with a proposition. 'My father would never forgive me if he didn't have the chance to meet you again, Mr Carter.' A twist of the key she'd withdrawn from a deep pocket in her dress, and the door opened. 'Come on in.' A final, fresh faced smile for the outlaw's leader, and she shut the door in his face.

'What was that about?' Zak's voice was far from gentle and his fingers dug into Sarah Jo's shoulders when he wrenched her around to face him.

'I was saving your worthless skin, Zachariah Carter. If I wasn't there, he'd have had you beaten, maybe even killed.'

'You were flirting with him,' Zak accused. He knew as well as she the man had meant him harm, but there was more to explain than that.

'He wants to marry me.' Sarah Jo was openly grinning at the expression on Zak's face.

'He wants to what?'

'Marry me! Is that so surprising?' The girl struck a pose that showed off her figure. 'I've grown up too,' she told him quite unnecessarily.

'That old bastard never wanted to marry anyone in his life.' Zak's tone echoed his lack of belief. 'Rape and murder are more in his line.'

'He does now.' Mr Mountjoy stood at the head of the staircase looking down at them. His face was pale but he was resolute. 'Please leave us now, Zachariah. I must speak with my daughter.'

★ ★ ★

Zak saddled his horse by the flickering light of a lantern given him by the stable lad. He'd left the banker's apartment without seeing hide nor hair of the Ghost Riders, and he assumed they'd repaired to the nearest bar until he entered the dark livery stable.

He knew straight away that his retreat had been cut off when one of the men closed the big, double barn doors, but he didn't lose his nerve. They'd come for him in their own time, that he knew, but he'd need his horse ready for instant flight if the opportunity arose.

So he got on with the job, his ears pricked to detect the faintest sound. How many men were there? One or two would be enough if they planned to shoot him down, but there was stealthy shuffling enough for half a dozen. A beating then! And he'd be lucky to survive that.

They came at a rush, more than he'd expected. His pistol sprung into his hand and he fired blindly into the dark depths of the livery, smiling wolfishly when one of them cried out in pain. The shadows melted into nothing and he set himself to spring into the saddle when something slammed against the side of his head. The pistol dropped from his nerveless fingers and he began to slump while they came on again.

6

Matters Come to a Head

Zak came to while it was still dark. He was laying in a proper bed, the mattress soft and yielding beneath him, the covers clean, crisp against his skin. He could sense Sarah Jo too, the warm scent of her, dozing in an overstuffed easy chair by his side. He attempted to shift, intending to settle more comfortably, and felt instead the throbbing agony of his wounds.

He'd been hit from behind, and the memory of that cowardly blow flooded back. Hit hard enough to stun him, he decided. His chaotic thoughts coalesced, and the odd flash of his other painful injuries intruded, echoing crazily in his consciousness; fuzzy dreams, never quite recalled, like wraiths in the night. The wooden haft from an axe arcing down from on high; heavy, leather boots thudding into his ribs; the agonizing slice of another's rowels. All that and much more flashed through his mind before he roused himself properly. Was he really awake, even now?

'Zak?' Sarah Jo's voice was tremulous. She'd been worried that he'd die before he emerged from his coma. Could be he still wouldn't recover, she reminded herself.

'Sarah Jo. How did . . . ?'

'Don't talk.' The girl could see the pain he was in, but she knew what question he was asking. 'Young Mike, the stable lad, brought the news to me. He sleeps up in the loft, amongst the hay and he heard them take you. He didn't know what to do, other than keep his head down, but he was brave enough to creep down and find you when the bully boys left. Saved your life, more than likely.'

'The Preacher!'

'When he saw who you were,' Sarah

Jo ignored Zak's interruption, 'he recollected that you knew me, and knocked us up. I was clearing away the supper dishes and answered the door myself; poor Father might have sent him away with a flea in his ear.

'I thought you were dead when I first saw you, but the lad found a pulse still beating and managed to pour a little brandy down your throat. You were a dead weight, too heavy to lift, but Mike and I dragged you across the street between us, and somehow managed to haul you up the stairs. I thought Father would have an apoplexy when he spotted us, but I convinced him it was for the best.'

'What about my clothes?'

'I'll wash them in the morning.'

'But — '

'We had to strip you so I could bathe your wounds.' Even in the faint light of a single candle Zak could see the blush creep into her face. 'It isn't as if I've never seen you bare before.'

Zak wanted to remind her it was a

long time since they'd shucked off their clothes and bathed together. That he'd grown up, but somehow it didn't seem to matter. He found himself floating away on a gossamer cloud of half remembered reminiscence, and whether he'd slipped into unconsciousness again or merely slept he never knew. His dreams were just as sweet either way.

When he came to properly it was light and his clothes, freshly laundered, were perched on the dresser at the foot of his bed. He had a dim recollection that he'd woken up several times in the past few days. Was it more or less than that? Sarah Jo had always been present; she'd nursed him back to health, but he couldn't recall whether anyone else had spelled her.

He decided he must have made a recovery, but when he made an attempt to sit up, he promptly revised his opinions. His head was thumping, spinning, and every bone in his body ached to the marrow. It was quite plain to him that he wasn't fit enough to sit, let alone stand. Then his native obstinacy kicked in and he forced himself into a sitting position, though the effort exhausted him in both mind and body. Good God, what would happen if the Preacher discovered him in this condition?

'You're awake again. Good.' Sarah Jo had slipped quietly through the door with a bowl of thin, steaming soup in her hands. 'If you drink some of this, it'll do you good.'

Zak held up a hand to take the bowl and promptly dropped it back to the coverlets. His right hand, his gun hand, was a livid purple bruise, swollen to twice its normal size, whilst his fingers resembled nothing more than over-stuffed sausages. As though the very thought could awaken the pain, his hand began to throb like he'd thrust it into the fires of Hell.

'There's no bones broken,' Sarah Jo assured him. 'Doc Jones looked you over yesterday. Lots of bruising, some of the worst he's ever seen, and a cracked rib or two. It's the blows you took to the head that worried him. They left you lying low and it's likely to take a week or two to heal even if you kept quiet.'

'I don't know Doc Jones.'

'He moved in two, three years back, after your time. He's a good man. He won't let on you're up in our attic room.'

'The Preacher won't like it.' Zak grimaced when the girl sat down and began to spoon the soup through his torn and bruised lips.

'I dare say you're right. Folks tell me he's in a rare taking, though none of them know the reason.'

Zak raised his eyebrows, wincing when even this small gesture awakened fresh pain from his wounds. No doubt his lifeless body should have been discovered by now.

'Has he admitted attacking me?'

'He was in the saloon all night, with witnesses enough to absolve him and all his gang.'

'I'll bet.' Zak winced again when he clenched his bruised and battered fists. 'What's between him and you?'

'Nothing.' A look of mulish obstinacy came over Sarah Jo's face before she confessed. 'He set out to woo me, even offered to marry me. Made the offer several times. I nearly spat in his face on the first occasion, but Father told me to go easy on him, so I just string him along for the time being.'

'The Preacher won't be patient forever.' A sudden dread seized Zak. 'He's the kind of man who'll take what doesn't come to him of its own accord.'

'I know how it is, but what can I do?' The dismay in her tone told Zak just how frightened Sarah Jo was, though she was too proud to admit her fear of the renegade's power, even to him.

'It'd be a comfortable life for the banker whose daughter married the only outlaw in the territory likely to rob him.' Zak drew a bow at random and was promptly disabused.

'You've misjudged my father.' Sarah

Jo stared back at him solemnly, abruptly recovering her habitual calmness. 'He may sometimes take his standing in society too seriously, but he'd never sacrifice his own daughter to maintain it. He's selling up his interests in secret, and we're moving away east as soon as he's done the deal. We have enough to establish ourselves handsomely in the city.'

'What the — '

A sudden crash of glass broke through their thoughts and Sarah Jo ran to the door to discover its cause. Her father was shouting down below and she held up her skirts and scampered down the stairs to join him.

'They've discovered you're here,' she told him shortly when she returned a few minutes later, 'and put a stone through one of our windows.' She stared in quiet contemplation. Zak Carter had dressed himself and was in the act of buckling on his gunbelt.

'Mike found your pistol on the floor of the stall your horse was in. No need to worry about the animal either, he'll have looked after it well.'

'Good enough. I'll need a fleet mount if I'm to ride out of town unharmed.'

'You're in no state to leave us yet.'

'I'll be dead if I don't, and so will you. Or worse.' He held up the bruised and swollen fingers of his right hand. 'I'm in no condition to defend myself, or to defend you.'

'He's right, lass.' The banker's deep voice took them both by surprise. 'He has to leave now, ready or not. Smashing our window was a warning we have to take seriously. If Zak Carter's still in town tonight then they'll be gunning for him.' He paused. 'The Preacher will soon be pressing you for an answer too. Don't antagonize him with an outright refusal, and be ready to leave as soon as my business is complete.'

7

A Surprise in Town

Zak Carter surveyed the girl's approach from a conveniently placed ledge above the makeshift cabin under the shadow of the bluffs. He'd been back in residence for nearly a week and his gun hand had recovered to the point where he could trust it to hold a pistol, but he was still too weak to move far from the old line hut his parents had built all those years before.

'I thought you'd be staying out here,' she greeted him cheerily, looking around at the preparations he'd made to defend himself. 'Do the Ghost Riders know where you're living?'

Zak hunched his shoulders in an unconcerned shrug. 'They may hazard a guess at my whereabouts, but so far as I know, they've never ridden around this part of the range. We're a fair distance from the canyon's main entrance and they're not the kind of men to explore for discovery's own sake.' He shrugged again. 'Sooner or later they'll find me. I won't be able to lay low for ever, not if I'm going to build up the ranch again.'

'I was worried they'd be out here waiting for you.'

'So was I.' Zak laughed mirthlessly. 'I was half dead of exhaustion by the time I reached the cabin, but I still staked it out for hours, laid out in the rocks, until I was sure it was safe to enter. I don't know why I bothered, I was in no state to fight even if they were waiting for me. No state to move on either. Come to that, you're a long way from town. What are you doing up here?'

'I guessed you might be getting low on provisions, so I stocked up for you,' Sarah Jo told him with a smile, indicating a small supply of sacks and boxes in the well of the buggy she'd driven. 'I packed a picnic too. That is, if you're not too busy to eat with me?'

'We'll take it down to the creek,' he offered.

'No thanks.' A delicate blush mounted her cheeks when she remembered the times they'd splashed through that particular stretch of water together, and just how little they'd worn. 'I can't stay long if I'm going to get back to town by nightfall, so we may as well eat here as anywhere.'

Zak held up his arms and she slipped off the high seat into their support, blushing again when he continued to hold her, his hands gently settling either side of her waist. She stared up into his face and saw his lips only inches away.

Was he going to kiss her? Then when he put her aside and busied himself unloading the supplies, a vaguely unnerving feeling of disappointment. She wasn't going to admit it out loud, but she'd have liked him to.

The picnic was a success. They were able to relax for the first time since

Zak returned to the territory, content in one another's company, without the past obtruding on their thoughts. The pair of them also, as though by some unspoken agreement, steered their conversation away from the trials and tribulations occasioned by the Ghost Riders and their formidable leader, the Preacher.

It couldn't last, and in the end Sarah Jo, swallowing hard, had to broach the subject closest to her thoughts.

'Father's completed his business dealings,' she began abruptly. 'We'll be leaving the territory in a couple of weeks.' She looked up at him in confession. 'It's a good time to make our escape, the Preacher called in this morning to tell me he expects me to accept his proposal by the end of the month.

'I wish you were coming with us, but there's a dance arranged in town this Saturday week.' She paused, willing him to accept. 'You should be fully recovered by then, and I'll be there. So if you want the chance to bid me fare-well . . . ' She let the offer hang in mid air, her eyes wide on the rancher's face.

★ ★ ★

It was late and the dance was already in progress by the time Zak Carter rode into town in his Sunday best. The chosen venue was on level meadow land a short walk beyond the old cemetery and he could hear the rollicking calls of the dance to the music of the fiddle, backed by banjo and guitar as he strolled down the path to the grounds. The scene was lit up too, blazing torches set all around, and an open fire over which several cooks too many were broiling an ox, scenting the air with the mouth-watering aroma of roasting meat. In the open arena in front of the musicians, the dancers were capering, the men huzzahing loudly while they swung their partners in the reel.

His eyes narrowed when he approached

close enough to identify the figures. Sarah Jo was already out on the floor dancing. No more than he'd expected since she was the prettiest girl in town, and far too young to sit it out amid such lively entertainment. What he hadn't anticipated was that the Preacher himself would be partnering her, and holding her much too close for the rancher's liking.

Damnation! Why the devil was that black-hearted outlaw allowed to parade openly through the town? Everyone knew his reputation for all he was acting like a law abiding citizen.

But though he was taken aback by the other's unexpected appearance, Zak promptly dismissed the half formed notion he should fade away and leave the field to his enemy. Instead, he threw discretion to the wind and strode across the dance floor to interrupt the couple.

'I believe this is the dance you promised me, ma'am,' he began, targeting the girl. Then, with a courtly bow towards the outlaw leader. 'I hope you'll understand my breaking in on you, sir. Only Sarah Jo has promised to share her picnic with me, and this may be our last chance to dance prior to eating.'

For a moment the outcome lay in the balance. The play of emotions displayed in the outlaw's face was very obvious to his audience, but with an effort he mastered his baser feelings and stepped back with a bow that matched his rival's in its formal courtesy, though his eyes glittered with a feral menace that wasn't lost on the rancher.

'I had hoped you'd take my warning seriously, Mr Carter,' he murmured under his breath when he turned away, so that only the rancher could hear. 'Next time you may not escape your fate so easily. Dance then, and eat heartily. Let the condemned man be merry while he still may.'

'What did he say?' Sarah Jo laid her hand lightly on Zak's shoulder and slipped into his embrace. If she was relieved to be rescued from the outlaw's arms then she schooled her face not to show it.

'Nothing of any real importance. Only an empty threat.' Ever since he'd returned to take up his inheritance, Zak had known there could be no turning back on his momentous decision. Girl or no girl, the lines had already been drawn, and sooner or later the Ghost Riders would be bearing down on his ranch to match their steel against his own.

'Be careful, Zak. He's a dangerous man to cross.'

'Has he been pressing you?'

'He wants an answer to his proposal soon, but he won't get the one he hopes for. If he pressures me too far tonight, I'll have no option but to decline, and tell him so right to his face. He won't dare force me into accepting his suit with all these people around, and with any luck that's the last I'll see of him. We'll be leaving the territory for ever later this week.'

Sarah Jo allowed her body to relax

closer into Zak's and laughed. 'Forget the Preacher, and dance with me tonight. Dance until the music stops. It may be our last chance.'

'It's already too late.' The young rancher frowned when the band stopped their music abruptly. 'Looks like the musicians are getting ready to eat. I'll find you a plateful too.'

'No, not yet.' Sarah Jo tossed her head restlessly. 'Walk with me for a while.' She slipped her arm under his and urged him towards the shadowed path that led past the cemetery and down to the church.

'What did you do out east?' Zak may have asked the question, but it wasn't the answer to that query he was really seeking. When a pretty girl invited a man to walk with her in the dark he would naturally think of romance. Did Sarah Jo think that way too?

'Father wished it. He wanted me to attend a select finishing school,' she returned in an abstracted manner. 'Told me it would improve my chances in life

85

if I completed my education.'

'He hoped you'd find a man to marry?' Zak made the translation easily enough. He knew the bank manager had high ambitions for his daughter.

'He would have been pleased as punch if I met my husband there. If he were the right kind of man, of course.' She laughed, her tone low and hollow. 'Poor father. The school was much too strict to encourage young men of any sort to dangle around its pupils.'

'Then you didn't meet a man?' The young rancher found himself feeling absurdly happy at the thought.

'I met several men at the formal dances the school organized, but no one special.' Sarah Jo found herself watching Zak's face to gauge his reactions. 'They were all too busy studying at a suitable college or carving out a career, and most of them had anything but marriage on their minds.'

'You were bored?'

She looked him directly in the eye and tacitly agreed. 'The west is my home, where I'm most comfortable. This town is where I've lived most of my life. I never realized how much I'd miss it until now. I never ever wanted to, not like Father, not until . . . '

They were treading on dangerous territory and Zak knew it. He still felt guilty about his betrayal of her love. Hell, he still felt guilty about leaving town, however desperate his situation had been, especially now he knew how tragically Tom Hardie had died.

'I was angry when you left,' she went on. 'I told myself you'd spurned me, that you'd chosen her over me, but most of all I was angry that you'd left town without me.' She turned towards him and grasped his arm in both hands. 'I would have gone with you, Zak, faced whatever troubles befell us so long as I was at your side.' Then, with a sob racking her voice, 'I still would, if you'd take me. I love you, Zak Carter.'

It was wrong and he knew it. He was facing the wrath of the Ghost Riders on his own, but he couldn't help himself.

He caught Sarah Jo in his arms and began to kiss her. Not the sweet, all but innocent kisses they'd shared in their youthful passion, but an open mouthed, willing, mingling of lips and tongues. He was a man now, and she a grown woman. If he felt any need to seek assurance on that, the way she twined her arms about his shoulders and thrust her body hard against his own would have proved it.

He growled deep in his throat and caught her closer, his hands moulding the curves of her body while he ravaged her mouth. Her breasts were crushed against his chest and he thrust aside the loose material of her gown, baring her shoulders to the depredations of his plundering lips, raining tiny, fluttering kisses down the sensual delights of the soft hollows revealed. Her scent was in his nostrils, his blood running hot and heavy, thudding through his veins, while his passions rose unchecked.

'We can't, Zak. Not here!'

Sarah Jo blushed scarlet when she

realized how her words suggested she would countenance his love making at the right time and place. Then blushed all the more fierily when she realized how easily her desire had matched his own. Oh, how much she longed for him to ignore her protests, to take her then and there before they were separated for ever.

Zak, however, controlled his eager passions with a visible effort and released her from his embrace. Her words had acted like a douche of cold water thrown in his face, dousing his smouldering desire; the fire wasn't out but it remained banked for the time being. Sarah Jo was his girl now, but she was right to call a halt. They were barely of sight of the other dancers, plumb in the centre of town. Her father would soon be out looking for her if they didn't return to the party, even the Preacher if his jealousy reached that far.

'I'll come for you,' he told her, gripping her shoulders. 'Wherever you are, I'll come, but not until I've settled accounts with the Preacher and his band of ruffians.'

The flickering flames burning in his eyes decided the girl and she made the bold suggestion in a shaky voice.

'Meet me by the creek at Scatterbone tomorrow, Zak. It'll be my last chance to see you alone.' She stared at him in trembling anticipation. 'Father and I will be leaving town on the early stage Monday morning, neither the Preacher, nor any other of the Ghost Riders is likely to be around to spot us at that time. Father's taken a house in Boston, I'll give you the address.'

★　★　★

They were laying for him when he left the brightly lit arena of the dance a couple of hours later. Sarah Jo and her father had left a few minutes earlier, but some of the wilder elements in town still partied on.

He strode slowly down the path

towards the church, his mind wandering back to the memory of the warm and willing woman who'd come to his arms on that very same route only a few hours earlier. Beside the church there was a narrow alleyway that led into Main Street and the livery where he'd collect his horse.

Deadly shadows shifted and coalesced in the dimly lit thoroughfare, and conscious of his danger, he flung himself full length on the ground. Two rifles fired as one, but his reflex action had disturbed their aim and both shells whined overhead. He scooped out his pistol with the assurance of long experience, and rolled rapidly into the thicker cover provided by a straggly patch of bindweeds that fronted the nearby graveyard. A single, penetrating glance was enough to show him the assassins were settling into the cover provided by the church, and aiming to shoot him down at long range, so he slithered across the low wall and melted silently into the dark, unlit

depths of the cemetery.

A further volley of shots rang out and he was dimly aware that the music of the dance had abruptly ceased. The remaining merry makers would be melting away into the night, only too anxious to avoid being drawn into a fire fight with the redoubtable Ghost Riders.

One of the outlaws opened up in a positive fusillade, spraying the cemetery with lead and covering his companion while he sprang forward, zig zagging in a low crouch towards the cover of the graveyard walls.

It was an unfortunate mistake, for the gunmen had underestimated their opponent. He wasn't running scared and neither had he needed to avoid their covering fire. Safely hidden by the dark of the night, Zak had long since shifted his position, silently closing in on the men who'd attacked him, seeking to shorten the range where he could make his handgun count.

He fired at the runner, still too far off

for accurate pistol shooting, but scored a direct hit. The man went down like a shot jack rabbit, rolled over twice, then flung himself into cover.

Zak knew better than to discount the man; he was wounded, but not badly enough to drop him in his tracks, and he still had hold of his rifle. He slid from shadow to shadow, crouching low to minimize his outline, and testing each footfall before he made it, his every sense alert for his opponents. The one closest to him was still moving despite his wound, creeping as carefully as himself, though not quite so silently.

He reached the low wall that bounded the cemetery and slithered over it, silent and deadly as a snake. The outlaw who'd provided the covering fire was still hidden in the alley, a darker silhouette against the lighter ground echoed from the streets behind. Zak took careful aim and fired, then made himself as small a target as possible in the angle of the wall, knowing he'd exposed his position to the man's companion.

He'd missed too. Shooting a pistol at extreme range on a dark night was a chancy business at the best of times! No second chances either — the alleyway was empty and the outlaw who'd inhabited it had disappeared into some hidden bolt-hole of his own.

He turned his attention back on the man he'd wounded, half aware the outlaw was creeping in the wrong direction to stalk him. Zak fired three times, fanning his pistol to hurry the bushwhacker on his way. A scrabbling of boots sank in, and the rancher abruptly realized the man was running. Running blind, for he was making for the arena marked out for the dance. The fire was still smouldering and he was briefly illuminated in its glare. There was no one else in sight and the young rancher fired off a final snapshot to hurry the outlaw along.

Shifting his position again, he reloaded his gun and settled down to wait his final enemy out.

Time dragged on without the man making an appearance, or even loosing off a snapshot of his own, but Zak still waited, his eyes concentrated on the entrance to the dark confines of the alleyway. He'd long ago learned the importance of patience; charging out into the open might have short-circuited the wait, but if the man were still in hiding it would leave his adversary with a clear shot at him.

At long last Zak decided the outlaw was truly gone, but, typically thorough, he slipped quietly through the grave-yard in a wide circuit around main street rather than risk providing a target in the narrow alleyway. Presumably the outlaw had retreated down that same alleyway, probably at the same time as his companion had run off, but it was as well to be sure.

8

Ambush at Scatterbone Creek

Following the attempt on his life the previous night, Zak was wary of the outlaws following him down to Scatterbone Creek for his assignation with Sarah Jo. Accordingly he set off early, and swung out in a wide detour across the prairie, where the flat pastures would provide precious little cover for any bushwhackers that still clung to his tail. A double back through a canyon on the edge of a rocky outcrop saw him overlooking his own trail, and able to double check the route for himself.

His backtrail was clearly visible over several miles from his elevated viewpoint and the landscape was empty so far as he could see, but he still waited patiently until he was sure before he heaved a sigh of relief. The day was hot, oppressively so, and he decided it must be the heat that ignited his anxieties. Either that, or the unspoken threat of the Preacher and his Ghost Riders. The outlaw chief wasn't well known for his patience and he'd be chafing at his lack of success, both in doing away with Zak Carter and of reeling in the girl.

'Hello Zak.'

Sarah Jo greeted the rancher almost shyly when he dismounted and tied his horse loosely to the back of her buggy. He hadn't gone so far as asking her to marry him, but there'd been a definite understanding between the two of them the previous night, and she was well aware of how bold her suggestion that they meet by the creek would appear. Especially since he'd kissed her.

'Sarah Jo.'

Zak realized his own reply was stilted, but he was as tongue-tied as the banker's daughter for the moment. She was leaving town the very next morning and he wouldn't see her again any time soon, perhaps not for several months, maybe even never if the Ghost Riders had their way. He wasn't usually nervous around women, he'd met them in just about every town he'd visited, but they were usually the type of girls who frequented the same saloons he did. Whores or, at best, women of dubious morals, while he was very aware that Sarah Jo was a lady whom he loved enough to treat as such.

'Take your boots off and join me,' she invited with a bewitching smile on her face, indicating a spot by her side. She was seated on a flat rock by the edge of the stream and dangling her bare feet into its cooling water.

Zak sat, his nostrils full of the scent of her, his shoulder touching hers, while his eyes weighed the slim perfection of her ankles and the well turned length of calf exposed where she'd hooked up her skirts to protect them from the waters.

They sat in companionable silence for several minutes, happy just to be alone together, but her imminent departure from the territory was preying on both their minds.

'Sarah Jo,' he began, though what he had to say was forgotten when she turned her head towards him and they made contact eyeball to eyeball.

It was as though they were looking into one another's souls, and when his arm shifted to slither around her shoulders, she subsided with a shudder into his body. Their lips met and she closed her eyes, shutting out any protests about the way her curves melded so closely against the whipcord strength of his body. His free hand met her rib cage, holding her still while he deepened the kiss, savouring the taste of her on his tongue.

She broke off the embrace long enough to curse when the hem of her skirt slipped into the stream and hooked it up again abruptly, pinning it firmly under her legs, while Zak gazed with ill-concealed interest at the length of smooth skinned thigh exposed.

Sarah Jo gave a mischievous grin

when she saw where he was looking, but she didn't attempt to cover herself, only encouraging him to look further while her arms slid around his broad shoulders, her fingers interlocking behind his neck. Half aware her tease was deliberate, he growled passionately, and hooking his free arm under her legs, picked the girl up bodily and deposited her on his lap. They were kissing again, and one sweet breast was nestling tremulously in his palm, his thumb flicking over the delicate nub of her nipple through the thin material of her blouse.

It wasn't enough and he began to unfasten the buttons down her bodice while she returned his open mouthed kisses with more and greater passion. His hand slid under her blouse, pushed aside the loose camisole beneath and settled on its prize. Her breast peaked beneath his caress and she instinctively arched against his body, offering her curves for him to plunder.

Their steamy kisses became more

passionate by the minute, his hands praising her figure while his body grew harder. Somehow his shirt had been peeled off his shoulders and Sarah Jo's hemline had retreated even higher up her thighs, when the first intimation that something was wrong hit him like a hammer blow in his belly.

Another rattle of stones, too close for comfort, decided him, and he reached for his pistol while he rolled with a swift intent that saw the pair of them plunged into the cool waters of the stream, lying prone under cover of the bank.

Sarah Jo shrieked out in alarm and tried to struggle free, but he held her down.

'Someone's stalking us,' he explained, and she stilled against his watchful body.

'I'm soaked through,' she murmured in his ear. 'Do we have to stay here?'

Zak was as wet as she, but he couldn't risk losing what shelter they'd gained, precarious though it was, until he knew where their pursuers were situated. And, more importantly, their intentions. They were hardly likely to be innocent, he decided, when they were creeping up so furtively.

A head suddenly appeared above the brow of the rocks further up stream, where a small waterfall gurgled over the edge of a short drop into the wide depression of Scatterbone Creek.

'Damnation! They've gone.' The disembodied head turned to speak to someone behind.

Zak drew a careful bead on the man, but he didn't shoot. Perhaps the men were innocent bystanders, though why an innocent man he didn't recognize should want to surprise them he couldn't imagine. In any case, while he had the girl in his charge, he owed it to her to find out how many opponents he might have to face before opening hostilities. So long as they could remain in hiding, she'd be safe.

'The Preacher ain't going to like it if we don't track her down.' A second man appeared from nowhere and settled himself beside the first, scanning the ground in front of them.

'They've gotta be somewhere close by. I heard the girl shout out a minute ago.'

'Yeah, that's right.' A third voice, its owner still unseen, joined in the conversation. 'She gave a shriek like that cowboy just stuck his hand up her skirts.'

'The Preacher won't like that either,' one of them decided.

Two of the men suddenly slithered over the rocks and stood in full view of the pair in the water.

'Hot damn, but she's a pretty little thing. No wonder the Preacher wants her so bad.'

This was Zak's first intimation that the men were after Sarah Jo, presumably to kidnap her, and not himself. They must have spotted her leaving town and followed at a distance. Set on to her by the Preacher, or so it appeared.

'There's a buggy back here, and a

horse too.' The previously unseen member joined the other pair and Zak wondered whether that was the sum of them. 'They ain't far off, and they're awful quiet. You don't suppose they're watching us do you?'

The outlaws, evidently three of the gang loyal to the Ghost Riders, made the connection at the same time Zak did: he was now the hunter and they the prey. He cut one down and fired twice more while they scattered, then surged through the water, drawing his companion in his wake.

The far side of the stream was a rock strewn embankment that promised better shelter and they flung themselves into its cover with their clothes streaming water.

'You hit a second one,' Sarah Jo told him calmly, shaking out her skirts. 'Bad enough to make him stagger, but not fatal.' She sounded disappointed.

Zak stared out across the stream. One of the outlaws was twitching spasmodically, laying on his belly out in

the open, evidently unable either to take cover or join battle. If he'd hit another bad, then the fight had swung their way unless there were reinforcements close by to bolster up their enemies' forces.

He made the decision on the instant. The longer he waited, the more likely it was the Preacher's men would arrive in force. Where there were three, he decided, then the others wouldn't be far off. And the gunshots already fired would draw them in.

'Stay here,' he ordered, and slithered along the rocky bank, heading upstream.

The waterfall was low, but it marked the edge of a small escarpment, only three or four feet high, over which the men had disappeared. It also provided him with the cover necessary to cross the stream, almost under their noses. They'd be expecting him to stay on the water's far side and his sudden appearance on the near bank might give him the edge he needed. He crawled into its depths, the water cascading over his body and soaking what little dry clothing still remained, but when he emerged he could hear their breathing.

One of them was hurt bad, for the breath was hissing through his teeth, evidently an attempt to stop himself from crying out loud.

'Hush your noise.' The other wasn't sympathetic. He'd been trying to locate Sarah Jo's position, assuming that the rancher would still be at her side.

'For God's sake don't hit the girl.' Zak heard the pain in the thin voice. 'The Preacher will kill us if we hurt her.'

'If we don't nail that damned rancher, he'll kill us first.' The other took a more pragmatic approach. 'Hold your noise, I think I see them.' He slithered forward with an obscene curse. Then stilled. He was looking straight down the barrel of Zak's pistol.

To his credit the man had courage enough to fight. He twisted lithely and tried to bring his own gun to bear, but it was all too late, and he died where he lay. The wounded man was on his own, but the bullet evidently hadn't affected his legs. He ran like a jack rabbit, and Zak was content to let him go.

★　★　★

Sarah Jo came to his arms and he embraced her gently.

'They were after you,' he told her shortly, ignoring the bedraggled state of her clothes. 'We're heading straight for town. Once you're back home, stay there until it's time for you to leave tomorrow morning. Don't abandon your father's protection for any reason whatsoever. If the Preacher ever held you captive up on the bluffs, you'd have precious little option but to accept his proposals.'

'Even the Preacher wouldn't go so far as that,' she ventured the opinion. 'Would he?'

Zak held her at arm's length. Her blouse still hung loose and the delicate material of the chemise beneath was

107

soaked through. Sarah Jo stared down at herself, shocked by the way her breasts were exposed by the transparent material. For just one moment she considered covering herself, then gave up. Let him look his fill. She was his woman, anytime he chose to claim her.

'I'll report to the sheriff as soon as we get to town,' the rancher decided. 'He can sort this mess out.'

His heart was beating faster, his libido not improved by Sarah Jo's state of undress. He wanted to claim the girl right now, take her back to his ranch and ravish her, but it could never be, not while he still had the Preacher to settle with.

9

The Abduction

Zak drove Sarah Jo back to town, staying by her side while she delivered the buggy to the livery stable and escorting her on the short walk around the back of the building that housed the bank. The entrance to the second floor apartment she shared with her father lay there, and they shared a quick kiss before she slipped inside, double locking the door behind her.

No doubt her father would wonder about the sodden, dishevelled state of her clothing, but he left it to the girl to explain matters to the banker and strode off towards the graveyard. Somehow he knew his battle with the Ghost Riders was going into its final furlong, and he decided to draw strength from his mother's grave for what might prove to be the last time.

The shooting began before he'd been at the graveside for more than a minute or two and he turned to stare down the narrow alleyway which led into Main Street. A man stumbled through its entrance and flattened himself up against a corner of the church building, staggering in wide-eyed fright when he spied Zak running towards him with a pistol in his hand.

'What's happening out there?' Zak stood beside the apprehensive newcomer, anxiously scanning the narrow alleyway when another couple of shots echoed down from Main Street.

'The bank's being robbed.'

'Robbed?'

'Yeah, it's the Ghost Riders. They've run amok, shooting up the whole town, killing anyone who gets in their way.'

Zak concluded the man wasn't thinking properly. There'd been several shots true enough, but not enough to justify a claim of wholesale homicide. Nor of an entire gang of Ghost Riders.

It sounded more like someone was engaged in defending the bank against a much smaller party.

'Are you hit?' He eyed the man's appearance doubtfully, unable to detect any sign of a wound.

'No sir, but I sure ain't going out there again until them damned outlaws leave town.'

Zak nodded and advanced cautiously down the narrow alleyway on his own, peering anxiously into the shadowed opening. The church building was set back a step or two from Main Street, no more than a hundred yards from the bank, but he still couldn't decide exactly what was happening.

A further shot echoed out, swiftly followed by two others, and he diagnosed at least two different weapons while he slipped into the street and took cover behind a convenient horse trough. The rifleman he'd spotted sheltering there turned wide eyes on him, the badge on his chest proclaiming his occupation.

'OK Sheriff, I'm on your side,' Zak reassured the lawman swiftly. 'What's happening?'

'There's a couple of them thieving sidewinders holed up in the bank. I got a deputy in the livery opposite, but he's pinned down, and every time I raise my head, it's like to get shot off.'

A bullet whined over the trough as though to collaborate his story.

'Are they from the bluffs?'

'I guess so. No one else is likely to mess in their back yard. Sure hope the Preacher ain't going to ride in with the rest of the gang! Not while I'm stuck out here in the open.' The sheriff looked nervously over his shoulder.

'I thought he led all their raids personally?'

'I thought so myself until this happened, but perhaps they've got over confident. They opened fire on me and my deputy before we even spotted them. Hell, we weren't looking for trouble, our patrol was just finishing.'

'Only a couple of men, you say.' Zak

pondered the thought for a moment. 'If the Preacher's in town too, it's strange he hasn't come to their aid.'

'Maybe it ain't the Ghost Riders after all. For all his faults, the Preacher never attempted to rob our bank before.'

'Is there a back way out?'

'There's a door that leads through to Mr Mountjoy's apartment, and his entrance is out back, but I can't cover all the exits with just the two of us. Besides they've left their horses out front.'

Zak chanced a peek over the rim of the trough and took a splinter in the cheek for his pains. Whoever was at work in the bank was a crack shot.

'There's only two horses out front.'

'Only two of the thieving coyotes in there, so far as I can tell,' returned the sheriff testily. He was able to count as well as Zak. 'They can shoot real good though.'

'Two men acting on their own isn't enough to take the bank by force of arms, especially in full daylight. Not when the sheriff's office is only a few yards up the street, and he's out on patrol. They must have been pure mad to shoot their way in, especially once they'd already alerted you.'

'Mad as coots, unless the rest of the gang decide to take a hand in the game.'

It was Zak's turn to look over his shoulder, even though he immediately refuted the sheriff's suggestion.

'If the Ghost Riders were intent on taking this bank you'd know all about it by now,' he declared confidently. Then frowned while he considered the options. Perhaps the bank raid was just a side show. He knew the Preacher wanted him out of the way. Had this pair of outlaws been detailed to keep the sheriff quiet while he was gunned down in a separate incident? If so, their plans had been stymied when he'd gone to the lawman's aid.

'They've gone awful quiet.' He raised his head cautiously and stared at the building in front of them.

Someone opened the door and stepped out warily, waving a white handkerchief at them. A teller by the look of him, and as there was nothing to suggest anything untoward, the rancher slowly drew himself to his feet.

A figure slipped out of the livery opposite and called the sheriff forward.

'Charlie's coming out,' he yelled, 'and it looks like he's alone. Them varmints must have slipped out the back way.'

'That's Jim, my deputy,' the sheriff confirmed Zak's suspicions. He too stood up and began to sidle closer to the bank, keeping close to the protection of the buildings that fronted the side walk.

Zak fanned out into the street, holding his pistol at the ready. The robbery had been aborted; all his senses told him so, but there was no point in taking unnecessary chances. The sound of galloping horses told him where the outlaws had disappeared to. They must have had spare mounts waiting around back.

'What's the damage?' The sheriff began to question Charlie, who was evidently the teller he appeared to be.

'None that I can see, Sheriff,' the bank employee replied promptly. 'I was busy working on the books when they broke in and took me captive. Set up a watch by the window and opened up soon as they saw you. I guess it was just pure luck you were on hand.'

* * *

When Sarah Jo heard someone beating on the front door, she wondered who it could be. She should have been busy at her last minute packing, but her meeting with Zak had left her vaguely dissatisfied with the notion of leaving town. Her father's feet clattered down the staircase to answer the peremptory summons, but she barely noticed, only staring into space with a dreamy look on her face. The gunfight had been frightening, but her overriding memory of their assignation was the thrill of his hands on her body, touching her where he would, and recalling that sensation still had the power to make her shiver with a barely suppressed passion.

Heavy feet ascended and the door opened. She stared wide eyed, scarcely able to believe her own eyes. The Preacher stood there, swaggering into her own living room.

'Good evening, Miss Mountjoy,' he began, with an attempt at urbane charm that entirely missed its mark. 'I trust your exertions today haven't tired you too much.'

'Mr Hallevisz!' Sarah Jo stared at the outlaw nonplussed. What the devil was he doing there? Not just to ask after her health, that much was clear.

She'd known the man for a couple of months, even been formally introduced to him on the occasion of her homecoming party, but greeting him had never given her so much pleasure as bidding him farewell. Quite apart from his sinister reputation, the Preacher had no redeeming features that she could discern. His face was as harsh as his life, usually formed into a frown as ferocious as his lifestyle, and carried a scar that twisted his thin lips into a cruel and permanent leer that seemed to celebrate the evil deeds everyone knew he was capable of. His notoriety hadn't been earned by good works, nor in refraining from criminal iniquity, and his life reflected his character, a catalogue of unredeemable wickedness. Neither he, nor anyone else, believed in his redemption.

Sarah Jo's father had warned her several times that the outlaw leader wanted to marry her, but she hadn't believed a word of it until the man himself had drawn her to one side and made his proposal in person. She'd refused him point blank, of course, but he'd merely offered her a smile and told her he'd be back when she'd had time to think on his offer.

'The pleasure is entirely mine, Sarah.' When he used her given name the girl felt as though something cold and slimy had settled on her body and she shuddered. Aaron Hallevisz wasn't the sort of man she liked to be alone with. Hell, she didn't like to meet him full stop. Where had her father disappeared to?

A movement caught her eye, and fear washed over the girl like the tide up a beach. The Preacher wasn't alone after all, he had a bunch of his outlaws with him, though they'd hung back at the entrance. And all of a sudden she realized her father wouldn't be joining them. Not then, maybe not ever!

'Perhaps the cat has got your tongue?' The Preacher was enjoying her torture, the girl realized. Knew too, he could sense the fear coursing through her veins and clouding her senses.

'Have you killed my father?' Fear for his life lent her the will to ask the question.

'Not yet.' The Preacher signalled to one of his men and the bank manager was thrown bodily into the room. 'Is that what's frightening you?' he purred.

'It was only that you startled me,' she told the outlaw, lifting her head proudly. 'I was deep in thought.'

'About my proposal perhaps? You promised to give me an answer tonight, did you not?'

'No,' she declared stridently, then abruptly aware of how alone she was. 'Yes, perhaps.' She attempted a smile, but it was all too obviously forced and he only laughed at her.

'You needn't worry yourself about it any longer,' he told her in a voice that was beginning to rasp. 'I have the solution to all our problems.'

'You do?' Sarah Jo couldn't think what he meant until he fished a loop of tough twine out of a capacious pocket in the tails of his dark frock coat.

'It makes a poor ring, but it'll have to do until we reach the bluffs.'

Sarah Jo gave a moue of dismay and attempted to twist out of his reach, but the Preacher had already laid hold of one of her hands and drawn her hard up against his body, grinning evilly at her expression of distaste.

'You will learn to like me,' he told her in a guttural and unpleasant voice. 'Once I have you safe on the bluffs, you will have no choice in the matter.'

The girl's free hand whirled in a round-house slap that he blocked with an ease that told her he'd expected no less.

'I hope you're always so passionate,' he mocked her, deftly twining the rope around one wrist while he caught the other in an iron grasp, 'for I'm an impatient lover.'

She spat directly into his face, then cried out in pain when he deliberately twisted her arms higher up her back than strictly necessary to make the knot fast.

'You may be spawned of a she wolf,' he snarled, cuffing her, 'but there's not a woman alive that can't be tamed. Believe me, I'll enjoy bringing you to heel once I've got you safe in my lair.' He clapped a dirty hand over her mouth to cut off her abortive cry for help and signalled one of the other men to gag her.

'Leave her alone, you fiend.'

Sarah Jo stared in horror when her father suddenly rushed forward to assist her. Then broke down and sobbed when his bravery went without its reward. The Preacher didn't even blink at the interruption, just drew his pistol and clubbed the man down.

'Bring her along,' he told a pair of the outlaws, 'and keep your filthy hands off her body. She's mine until I tire of her.' The Preacher kept his pistol in his hands and a wary eye on the street outside. If anyone was going to mount a rescue, it would come from that direction.

* * *

A few minutes later Zak found himself lounging in the shadows that fronted the saloon opposite the sheriff's office, where that worthy was holding a public meeting, flanked by his deputy and the bank teller. His declared aim of taking off after the outlaws wasn't going down at all well with the men in town.

'See here, Sheriff; it ain't no use in setting up a posse,' one of the men argued. 'We all know those two belong to the Ghost Riders, Charlie recognized both of them. Jim too.' The meeting wasn't large, but the speaker still hung back, attempting to make himself as anonymous as possible.

'They were members of the gang right enough,' the sheriff's deputy agreed with a nod.

'Then the Preacher ain't likely to let us take them without a fight, whether he planned the raid or not. You know what he's like; he'd see us shot up as soon as look at us if we set ourselves up against him. If those men weren't acting under his orders then he'll deal with them himself. He won't risk any member of the gang undermining his authority.'

'There weren't nothing taken anyhow,' chimed in another sarcastically. 'Not from the bank, nor anywhere else. Since when has nothing been worth risking our lives for?'

'We could go to the federal marshal for help.' The sheriff, for once, seemed anxious to take a stand against the gang, possibly fearful for his own safety if the outlaws continued to target the town.

'That's a full day's ride, Sheriff. Tell the marshal there was no robbery, and he'd laugh in your face. You may have time to waste on a fool's errand, but I haven't.'

'This is the first time they've had a try at our bank,' the sheriff attempted to work on their fears. 'If we leave it be, then they'll know we're sitting plumb in the palm of their hand.'

'They know it already.'

The last remark was tempered with sarcasm, but it still earned a chorus of agreement from the other townsfolk.

'We've got enough trouble to deal with here in town without stirring up a hornet's nest up on the bluffs.'

'Maybe we ought to wait for more

evidence,' another suggested. 'It'd be plain foolish to move against the Ghost Riders if those men were acting of their own volition.'

Another chorus of agreement and it looked as though the sheriff would have to cave in. Zak suspected he wasn't too keen on leading a posse against the Ghost Riders anyway, not if he was expected to force their camp at Shotgun Bluffs with the meagre resources available in town. He'd probably been prompted into calling the meeting by the bank manager himself. That old skinflint always had been driven by cold, hard cash. Though why he should bother when he was leaving town the very next day was more than the rancher could imagine.

'Sheriff.' The bank manager himself suddenly sprinted down the street and joined in the argument, gasping breathlessly from his unfamiliar exertions.

'Mr Mountjoy.'

The sheriff stared at the unexpected arrival of the banker, whose face was a gruesome mask of dried and matted blood. The man may have been left breathless from the long run up the street, but he was determined to say his piece.

'It's my Sarah Jo, Sheriff. She's been kidnapped.'

Zak's air of nonchalance changed on the instant, and he stepped forward, his voice harsh.

'Who's taken her?'

'The Preacher! He beat on my door, backed by a full dozen of his desperadoes. I tried to stop them, but they pistol whipped me and when I came to, Sarah Jo had been taken.'

Zak cursed his hasty action in joining the sheriff in relieving the bank. He'd wondered whether the abortive raid was only a side show at the time, and now he realized just how right he'd been. It never had been intended as anything more than a feint, drawing off anyone who might be prevailed upon to put up a fight. The Preacher was a cleverer strategist than he'd ever given him credit for.

'Has he tried anything like this before, Mr Mountjoy?' The sheriff asked the question.

'She was attacked this very morning while out riding, but I never thought the Preacher would dare to abduct the girl from her own home, right in the centre of town.' The bank manager seemed stunned by the crime, as well he might be considering the bloody wounds on his own head. Zak knew that Mountjoy loved the girl. He may have been a skinflint in anything to do with money, but he'd never skimped on his daughter. She was his only child, everything he had, and he'd spoiled her accordingly.

'Why didn't you tell me about the attack this morning?' the sheriff asked fretfully.

'I was on my way to inform you myself, Sheriff,' Zak butted in, 'when I was decoyed by the raid on the bank, same as you. Those devils must have gone around the back door, while we were fooled into besieging the front.'

'I'll send Jim off to fetch the federal marshal straight away, Mr Mountjoy. The decent folk of this territory will raise merry hell over the kidnapping of an innocent young girl from her own home.' The sheriff stared around the crowd as though daring them to gainsay him, but their mood had changed with the news. Sarah Jo was a popular figure in town, always had been, and kidnapping a decent woman was abhorrent to them all.

'We'll mount our own posse too,' he stared out into the gathering shadows of evening doubtfully. 'We'll ride out tomorrow at first light, every damned one of us. That'll give us the chance to call in some of the ranchers and their cowboys too. Go get your guns boys, the Preacher's gone too far this time.'

'Too far indeed,' agreed Zak quietly, speaking for himself. He drew back from the crowd and began to pace down the street towards the livery. The Ghost Riders would have stolen a lead on him, but by no more than a mile or two. The sun was beginning to set, and the outlaws would have to make camp unless they rode through the darkest part of the night.

He growled in frustration; if the Preacher wanted the girl that badly, then he'd camp out and take her that very night. He'd never had much of a reputation for patience.

10

The Camp by The Bend of The River

Zak Carter saddled his horse and slipped quietly out of town, patiently negotiating the back alleyways so nobody would notice his departure. The less anyone knew of his immediate plans, the better he'd be pleased. The Preacher wasn't such a fool as not to have left his spies in town, and the rancher wanted to give no one the opportunity to creep up on him from behind.

No doubt the sheriff was only doing his job when he decided to wait until morning before giving chase. The posse would be all the stronger for calling in the local ranchers, but on the other hand, Sarah Jo's case would be the all the more desperate for the delay. If one man could make a difference to the girl's position, then Zak determined it would be him.

He laid out the lie of the land in his mind as he rode, and made his decision with quiet confidence. There was a convenient spot by a bend in the river, several miles out of town. Far enough for the outlaws to consider themselves safe from immediate pursuit, yet not so far they couldn't reach it in less than an hour or two. Thereafter the trail entered a much wilder part of the country, a terrain not so easy to traverse in the dark of the night.

The Ghost Riders would make their camp there, he reasoned. Men of their stamp wouldn't continue to ride through the night unless they had a much better reason to expect an immediate chase. They'd probably set a watch on the backtrail anyhow — there was a stand of cottonwood on the edge of an escarpment that was made for such an ambush. The Preacher too, had reasons of his own to break their flight. He wasn't a patient man and he had Sarah Jo in his power, far too tempting a morsel for his delectation to consider a hurried and uncomfortable journey through the night.

His decision made, Zak put his plans into action, urging his mount off the well worn trail and on to the rough prairie country that bounded it. He'd leave the spoor left by the outlaw's flight and circle about, bypassing any attempt to ambush him, and come on the camp from an unexpected direction. There was no moon that night, and it would be strange indeed if he couldn't get close enough to douse the outlaw chief's ardour, for a night at least.

His ride was a tough test for both man and beast. He was off the trail, often in thick undergrowth, then again in the broken, rocky terrain of a low range of hills, then skirting the banks of a deep, fast flowing river. The route he only barely recalled from long days of exploration in his youth, but he rode it now with the determined steadiness of a man full grown. A man, moreover, who'd experienced worse in his recent history, when he'd braved the most bizarre extremes of climate and terrain to ensure the security of the loads in his charge. Half remembered landmarks and a nose for seeking out his direction finally won him through, and he ended up laying prone in the reeds on the bank of a river, staring across the dark expanse of water at the outlaws' preparations to camp.

They'd made their halt at the bend as he'd expected; not much of a gamble seeing as how it was the perfect spot from the Ghost Riders' point of view. The swirl of the waters had eaten away the far bank, from where he lay watching, but more importantly left a wide, dry beach on their own side, close to, but not adjoining the main trail which disappeared into the depths of the forest close by. The going then would be hard indeed by night; the little used trail ran directly through the trees and hence its path would be tenuous even in daylight, and almost impossible to follow in the pitch black of a moonless night under the shadow of the leafy boughs.

The outlaws had already built up a fire and, while a couple were busily toasting dried bacon and bread on a blackened and greasy skillet, the others had settled themselves around the campfire, laughing and joking amongst themselves. Close by, and further down the beach, a makeshift tent had been constructed by throwing a blanket over an arrangement of poles to give their prisoner a little privacy. Zak could see the girl's pale face in the light of the lamp she'd been allowed and he growled under his breath. It wasn't her privacy the Preacher would be thinking of, it was his own, for he'd be planning to take her that very night.

So far as the rancher could make out, Sarah Jo hadn't been harmed in any way. It was too far off to spot whether she was sporting any bruises, though he could see her plainly in the entrance of her temporary abode. She was sitting straight, with her head erect and unbowed, apparently none the worse for wear. Next to her, a strong, freshly cut stake had been hammered into the ground, to which he suspected she'd been tethered.

While he silently watched, she swivelled her head warily from one side to the other, as though seeking the inspiration and opportunity for flight. Then she shook her head sadly when she realized that escaping her fate that night was an impossible task. Even in the dark of the night Zak could see there was a guard set, the ruddy firelight picking out the craggy features of his grizzled face and glinting on his watchful eyes. He stood some little distance from the girl, holding a rifle in the crook of his arm, set to guard the open ground between her and the river and block her only possible escape route, since she'd have to pass the main body of the outlaws to reach the trail.

There'd be other guards out too. Zak narrowed his eyes and stared into the dark depths of the camp, far outside the range of the blazing fire, but the pickets had been too cunningly concealed for him to spot them in the dark. No matter, it was the Preacher himself he needed to keep a watch on. And the Preacher was in plain sight over by the fire, helping himself to a sizzling platter of bacon. The rancher settled back and prepared to wait for his chance. Seizing the girl from under their noses was plainly impossible while she was so closely watched, but circumstances could and would change.

* * *

The Preacher waited until he'd consumed a leisurely meal before he set out in the direction of the girl with a confident leer disfiguring his face. Several of the men around the fire laughed out loud, and one, more daring then the rest, risked making a coarse quip to a chorus of catcalls, abruptly cut off when the outlaw chief turned on his audience and snarled a feral warning.

Zak, who found nothing funny in the situation, thrust forward his rifle and waited patiently for the man to approach Sarah Jo. He was caught in a cleft stick, for he didn't dare risk a shot to kill the man, even if he could have guaranteed the accuracy of his aim at long range in an uncertain light. The outlaw chief, for all his faults, was the only barrier that stood between the girl and the uncertain mercies of the debauched band of outlaws. Leave him dead or dying and the girl would be lost for sure, for while they remained in open country, he couldn't hope to snatch her from under their guns. Nevertheless, he was confident in his ability to ensure her safety for a night at least, and he prepared to enter into battle, slowly shifting his rifle so its barrel shadowed the Preacher's steady advance.

Any remaining hopes that the outlaw chief might be prepared to wait for his wedding night were blown away as soon as he joined the girl. The Preacher's patience was at an end. He faced her with an evil smirk and rapped out a command that Zak couldn't hear, though its meaning, if not its content, became obvious when Sarah Jo crossed her arms protectively across her bosom. The outlaw laughed out loud, a harsh cackle that grated on the rancher's ears, and he reached forward to touch her.

Zak fired on the instant. It was a warning shot, meant to whistle over the Preacher's head, but he evidently hadn't judged its trajectory correctly, for the lamp hanging off the makeshift tent erupted, and flung its flaming fuel in a dozen different directions.

Then everything seemed to happen in a single cataclysmic moment. The outlaw leader fell over backwards, startled as well he might be; the blanket that made up the tent's body flared up in a sheet of flame; the outlaws around the fire dived for cover in a panic stricken mass; and Sarah Jo flung herself full length on the ground.

Zak fired again, and straight away shifted his position, moving downstream. With his second shot he'd targeted the main body of the outlaws and he realized they would return fire as soon as they'd recovered from the shock. He was right, and a dozen guns opened up, though as most of them were using their pistols, none of the flying bullets came anywhere near him.

The Preacher had disappeared, though Zak could still hear him cursing. No doubt he'd swiftly worked out he was silhouetted by the fire while he remained close to the girl and adjusted his position accordingly, knowing with the uncertain light that the smallest fold in the ground would suffice to hide him. Sarah Jo was still tethered to her stake, but she'd shuffled away from the flaming ruins of her makeshift shelter and laid herself flat to the ground as low as she could get.

The rancher wasn't finished yet either. He crept along the river bank and targeted the lone guard. He too had disappeared, creeping out of the telltale light of the fire, but Zak had a good idea of his direction and swiftly pumped two shells into the darkness, ignoring the confused and isolated shots from the far bank. He knew he was in good cover, and the outlaws' lack of success in targeting him, despite their weight of fire, informed him they hadn't yet tracked him down. Small wonder, when most of them had yet to recover from the shock of suddenly coming under fire themselves.

The Preacher roared out a terse command and the shooting ceased abruptly, leaving Zak free to shift his position again. The outlaws' numerical superiority counted for nothing until they had him targeted. For all their numbers, it would have been suicide to storm his position in the dark of the night with the firelight illuminating them and a deep, swift flowing river to cross. They wouldn't dare do without the firelight either, not only would it have been difficult to douse the roaring flames, but an enemy taking occasional pot-shots at long range was infinitely preferable to the same man running amok in their midst. He'd be able to shoot at will, whereas they'd be constrained to identify their target before they fired!

It was an impasse, at least until daylight dawned. Then it would be the rancher at a disadvantage. Superior numbers would soon tell once the outlaws could see their enemy, pin him down and outflank him. Zak had no intention of waiting around for that to happen, stymying the Preacher's immediate plans for his future bride was his only ambition. They'd ride on early the next day, and with the probability of a posse following on their heels as soon as the sun rose, the outlaw chief wouldn't stop to consummate his prize until they were safely ensconced on Shotgun Bluffs.

The night passed slowly, but few of the participants managed any sleep. The rancher fired only occasionally, but it was enough to leave the outlaws skittish, their own returning shots spraying the river bank randomly and quite ineffectually. And by the time the new day eventually dawned, Zak was already in the saddle, confident Sarah Jo would remain safe for the day, while he rode his lonely trail and left the worsted outlaws to retreat to their bastion on the bluffs.

11

Shotgun Bluffs

The climb up to the bluffs was far harder than Zak could ever remember it. Of course he'd only been twelve years old when he last clambered up the bluffs, full of the optimism and agility of youth. Now he was a full grown man and trusting his weight to the sun blasted slopes of a mountain that all too often crumbled under his bulk.

He'd left his horse in the old corral that lay in the lee of the old line hut and walked to the start of the secret paths that led up to the bluff's back entrance. The old cattle trails at the foot of the cliffs had proved easy enough, but as he climbed higher and the way grew steeper, he began to labour under the heat of the rising sun, further distracted by the awkward bulk of the rifle slung across his back. Nevertheless, and despite the passage of time, he was sure of his directions, aiming steadily for the notch in the bluffs where the hanging valley spawned the series of spectacular waterfalls that surged down the cliffs to feed the creek far below.

He was within touching distance of his destination a little before noon, when he settled back at the foot of a final, almost vertical, climb, to listen for any hint the way might be guarded. It had been a long time since he climbed into the valley, and who knew how many secrets the outlaws had discovered in that period.

Predictably he could hear nothing but the constant gurgle of water escaping down the mountainside, and swiftly realized he would have to leave everything to blind chance. He went up the vertical incline at a run, scrambling noisily on the bare, rocky slopes and diving with precipitate haste over the rim, scrabbling for his pistol. That no enemies were laying for him was an anticlimax that left him feeling almost foolish until he saw the guard house.

Evidently the outlaws had considered the hanging valley worth guarding at some time in the past. Zak levelled his pistol on the shattered doorway and surveyed the building with distaste. The walls were crumbling and the most part of the roof had collapsed into the interior. It looked as though the hut hadn't been used in years, but, typically thorough, he searched through the ruin to confirm that fact. The Colonel, he considered, had been a soldier, one who would have insisted on the discipline of a guard, which his successor evidently thought unnecessary. Or perhaps, with the Preacher away in town so often, the remaining outlaws had become sloppy and disinclined to take on such duties.

No matter, the way was unguarded, and Zak began to trudge slowly up the valley floor, keeping well in the lee of what little cover was available. He clambered up what looked like a long disused path beside a tinkling waterfall, and exited on to the floor of the central valley with a suddenness that took his breath away. Perspiring heavily in the summer sun, he promptly sank down to survey the terrain.

The view before him had changed considerably since he last stood in that very same spot. There was still a lake in the very centre of the valley spawning the babbling brook that fed the waterhole in the hanging valley, but a township had sprung up on its near bank, close enough for him to clearly see its occupants. Closest to him were the outlying shacks, varying in the scale of their architecture and finish, but evidently occupied by members of the gang and their dependants. In the spaces between he could see several slovenly women, squatting in little groups to gossip, or simply cooking over open fires. Further off, two heavily bearded men were sat playing dice on a makeshift porch, a wide lipped brown jug placed between them, from which they took turns to swig its contents, presumably home distilled rot-gut whiskey.

In the centre of the shanties, a larger, more ambitious, but still single storey building had been erected. From its style Zak guessed it might serve as a barracks and cantina for the camp. A couple of horses were hitched to the rail in front of it, and a young, doe-eyed whore sprawled outside in her petticoats.

Further off there were other scattered buildings, perhaps two or three in all. One that took his eye was built in a much more elaborate style, in pale washed adobe, with a wide, covered porch overlooking the lake. Zak was guessing, but this house might have been part of the Colonel's domain until his death. Perhaps the Preacher had taken up residence there now, or maybe he had his rooms in the cantina.

No point in wasting time in such idle speculation, he told himself with a sigh, and began to look further off towards the far end of the valley. It was there that the canyon entrance exited into the valley, and by this time the outlaw gang and their prisoner must be negotiating its narrow maw.

He stood up with casual confidence, and began to stroll openly across the plateau, noting what landmarks he could, particularly those that would hide a fleeing man. His reasoning was sound, he considered; he would appear far less conspicuous if he acted as though he belonged there, rather than scurrying furtively from cover to cover. Several of the outlaws riding with the Preacher might recognize him since their contretemps in town, but it was unlikely that any of those remaining in the valley would. Not that anyone seemed at all interested in the lone figure anyway.

The outlaw cavalcade rode into the valley while he was still some distance from the entrance. The first inkling he had of their arrival was a sudden appearance from one of the guards set over the entrance, who stood tall and waved a rifle over his head. Whether this was meant as a greeting to the returning gang or a signal to the makeshift township, Zak neither knew nor cared. Grateful for the warning, he settled back into the shadow of an overhanging rock and prepared to watch the new arrivals.

The Preacher was in the van of the returning party, and as soon as he reached the plateau he began to allocate additional men to the defences. Evidently he hadn't discounted the possibility that the abduction of his prisoner might provoke a serious attempt at pursuit. Sarah Jo, herself, followed on in the centre of the procession, with two alert gunmen riding close by, evidently detailed to guard her. And once the outlaw chief had sorted out his dispositions, she and her escorts were dispatched, along with two slatternly women who'd arrived to meet the returning outlaws, to the adobe hut he'd already mentally labelled as the Colonel's residence.

Having no interest in the remainder of the band, Zak followed on at a safe distance, and watched dispassionately while the girl trailed dejectedly into the building, followed by the two women, who were evidently detailed to be her jailers. One of her male escorts took off with the horses while the other set himself on the porch outside, leaning nonchalantly against the door jamb. With the remainder of the outlaw band all around, Zak decided at once that all thoughts of rescue would have to be banished for the time being. While the Preacher was busy elsewhere, the girl should be safe enough, and he could review his plans if the situation deteriorated.

Keeping his movements nonchalant and his hat pulled well down over his eyes, Zak began to scout surreptitiously around the makeshift prison. The porch ran along the entire front elevation and contained the only door, left slightly ajar, with an open window immediately beside. The only other window, as he shortly discovered, was to the rear, a fixed pane set high and too narrow to admit a child, let alone a full grown man. Nevertheless, by climbing a slight prominence behind, he found he could stare through it, and into the room it guarded.

Sarah Jo, herself, wasn't in view, but he could plainly see how the building was divided into two rooms, connected by a wide arch, through which the partly open door was visible. One of the women, at least, was occupying the outer room, and presumably the other also, for the one he could see was evidently speaking. From all the evidence he could muster, Zak surmised the girl had been left alone, imprisoned in the inner room.

From his high viewpoint he could also see on to the flat roof, and the blackened maw of the low, wide chimney at its centre, big enough to admit a man as he calculated. Confident he'd found his way in, he settled back to await further developments.

It was late afternoon before Zak spotted his opportunity. The two women emerged from the interior to catch the late afternoon sun on the porch, and fell into casual conversation with the guard, who'd long since laid down his rifle and settled himself comfortably on to one of the chairs.

The rancher seized on the chance offered and, swiftly approaching the building from the rear, vaulted athletically on to the roof, where he crept across to the chimney opening. It wasn't as wide as he would have liked, but by sacrificing his rifle, holster and pistol, he found he could just squeeze through the narrow opening and wriggle down. It wasn't as speedy or as silent a rescue as he would have liked, since half way down he came across a kink in the chimney where it divided to provide a fireplace for both rooms, which had him stymied for a while. There he had to abandon his stealthy approach, arch his body and kick, writhing lithely in the confined space, and just when he thought he'd be stuck forever, skidded down into a tall, wide fireplace.

Sarah Jo was sitting on the bed with her arms stretched around behind her and evidently bound, but she must have been alerted to Zak's presence by the noise he'd made, for she didn't look in the least amazed by his sudden appearance. Just shook her head in a barely perceptible movement and rolled her eyes towards the arch that led through to the outer room. The rancher stilled in the fireplace, listening to a new voice gruffly issuing commands to the guards outside, and a moment later saw the man himself when he strode through the arch and approached the girl with a purposeful air.

Zak stiffened and looked around for a weapon. The outlaw had only to turn around and he'd see him standing in the ashes with no gun to defend himself with.

'Get up, girl, the Preacher wants to see you.'

'What if I won't?' The girl gave the outlaw back, stare for stare, her head held proudly, and the rancher realized she intended to keep the man's attention on herself to give him a chance.

'You'll go,' the man growled. 'Even if I have to carry you. The boss is anxious to get you wed and into his bed.' He stared at her, blatantly appraising her curves, 'and I sure don't blame him.'

'I'd rather throw myself off the bluffs than marry that evil old man.' Sarah Jo shuffled back on the bed as though shrinking away from her fate, but in fact, intent on making as much noise as she could to cover Zak's own movements. He'd already slithered stealthily out of the fireplace, his eyes firmly fixed on the outlaw, while he groped for his knife.

'You'll marry him, willing or not,' ground out the outlaw, and strode forward to catch hold of her with a shake of his head. 'The Preacher must be in love, or in his dotage, or he wouldn't bother with the ceremony.'

'How can we be wed?' Sarah Jo pleaded. 'There's no parson on the bluffs, and if there were, then he'd damn you all to hell.' She raised her tone an octave or two and tried to inject an air of hysteria into her voice. 'If he didn't damn himself first.' The imprisoned girl could see Zak creeping up behind the man with his knife pushed well to the fore, and knew she had to play her part to retain the man's concentration on herself.

'Clerics can be tempted too far themselves,' the outlaw reminded her, chuckling nastily. 'This one ain't likely to damn anyone to hell, least of all himself. Why should he, when drink or the devil will see him there all too soon.'

'My father will have every lawman in the country on the Preacher's tail. Yours too.' The girl tried another tack, facing up to her tormentor bravely. Zak was almost on him!

'They already are.' The outlaw gloated, and reached out to capture her, his patience at an end.

'Please,' she wailed. 'Let me go.' She licked her lips nervously and arched her body in an invitation he couldn't misinterpret. 'I'd be very grateful.'

The outlaw laughed out loud, evidently amused by his prisoner's offer, then suddenly stiffened.

Had he heard the rancher's stealthy approach? Or was there some flicker in the girl's eyes that warned him something was wrong? Whatever the reason, he turned, going for his gun with the instinctive reaction of a gun fighting man. The weapon slid easily out of its holster at the same moment Zak's last minute charge crunched into his body and loosened his grip.

Carried over by the rancher's momentum, the two men toppled back across the bed still battling with each other, while the pistol clattered uselessly across the floor. The outlaw realized he was fighting for his life and hung on to Zak's knife arm with a relentless determination, then flung his weight suddenly sideways, throwing them both off the bed, and giving the badman his opportunity. Taking immediate advantage of their temporary separation, and realizing his pistol was too far off to be safely retrieved, the outlaw made a dive for the doorway, roaring for help.

He passed through the opening a moment before Zak's knife thudded uselessly into its jamb.

★   ★   ★

Realizing the outlaw would quickly rally the guards outside if the commotion didn't, Zak swiftly retrieved his weapon and sliced through Sarah Jo's bonds. She flung herself bodily into his arms, but this was no time for hesitation and he thrust her gently away.

'Follow me,' he told her, and picking up the outlaw's gun, headed for the door just as the guard clattered in from the porch. The man's rifle was already levelled, but he evidently didn't know quite what to expect and Zak fired first.

The man went down heavily, losing hold of his weapon, but still able enough to scramble out of their way.

Seeing the man had no intention of drawing his pistol, Zak ignored him, only seizing the rifle as he passed through the doorway and flinging it to Sarah Jo, who was hot on his heels. Out on the porch the two women were cowering terrified at the far end, while the remaining outlaw was racing rapidity for the main township, hollering at the top of his voice.

Several of the outlaws were already staring at the commotion and, since it was obvious their route to the hanging valley would be cut off before they reached any sort of cover, Zak set off around back of Sarah Jo's temporary prison. During his earlier survey of the valley, he'd marked down a small islet, that consisted of no more than a jumble of rocks near the far end of the lake, and he was confident they'd make it that far without unduly exposing themselves to their enemy's fire.

12

Escape Route

Despite his initial confidence, Zak soon began to realize that escaping from the midst of their enemies wasn't going to be as simple as he'd calculated. Even fleeing the short distance to the rocky islet was a calculated risk, and its shelter dubious since he'd only surveyed it from a distance.

The pair came under fire when they took to the prominence behind the building, racing up its steep incline like bats out of hell. The scree strewn slope at its far side was a precipitate scramble, bedevilled by the shifting ground beneath their feet. Nevertheless they were thankful they were at last out of sight of the rapidly mobilizing band of badmen from the township who would otherwise have been in easy rifle range.

Two startled outlaws, presumably returning from picket duty on the canyon entrance, confronted them when they raced across the valley beyond, but evidently didn't understand the situation or its urgency. Zak's pistol exploded a moment before Sarah Jo backed him up with the rifle, and they went down, though whether they were hit or simply taking cover, the rancher never had time to decide. They were now in direct line of sight of the main outlaw bunch chasing them and beginning to come under fire again themselves. Zak caught hold of the girl's hand and ran on, randomly zig-zagging to put off the brigands' aim.

The rocky islet was neither high nor very extensive, but it provided cover enough for two, and given that the final sprint, splashing through the shallows, had exhausted both of the fugitives, they were grateful for any small mercy. Flinging themselves down, they lay supine, squirming into the gravel that filled in between the bigger rocks, until Zak, tiring of being a target, raised his head and snapped off a couple of shots of his own.

The more adventurous of the outlaws had been racing for the lakeside, but the sudden realization their quarry had teeth of their own drove them into cover too. And, as the firing died down, Zak stared around, satisfied with their position for the moment. They were trapped, but it was a trap their tormentors would find hard to spring while daylight lasted. Their shelter may not have been extensive, but it commanded a wide aspect of the lakeside, and any attempt to assault them directly would be suicidal.

His eyes searched further off too, while he took advantage of the lull to reload his pistol. There was nowhere close by that could overlook them, but the canyon walls rose much higher further off by the canyon entrance. Extreme rifle range, but a sharp shooter might make things uncomfortable for them if the Preacher was prepared to risk Sarah Jo falling victim too. He could hear that worthy taking charge of the siege, and decided that risking the girl was a step the outlaw chief would only take as a last resort, given what trouble he'd already undertaken to abduct her.

Sarah Jo's lithe body suddenly slithered closer, lying prone next to him; he could feel the heat of her body through his clothes.

'Here,' he told her, searching through his pockets for a handful of shells. 'That's all I've got.'

'Thanks.' She wasn't thanking him just for the shells and he knew it. 'I didn't think I'd ever escape that brute. Was it you that ambushed us by the river too?'

He nodded and she stretched and shifted to plant a kiss on his lips. It wasn't sexual, but it held a promise. A promise of nothing if he couldn't get them out of the valley, he reminded himself.

'How'd you get up here?'

'There's a path that leads up to a hanging valley the other side of their town,' he told her, and explained the route in greater detail. Perhaps she'd be able to escape off the plateau even if he were shot down. With any luck he could provide the sort of diversion that would give her a decent prospect of doing just that!

'What are our chances?'

'We're pretty secure while the light lasts,' he assured her, though he was perfectly sure she'd already worked that one out for herself.

'Not so good if they rush us at night then,' she concluded.

'Not if we remain here,' he agreed. 'As soon as it's dark enough to decamp safely, we'll move on. Given a slice of luck and no moon, we'll give them the slip yet.'

'There's still a couple of hours to go,' she commented and slithered closer, laying half across his body while she ran her fingers through his hair.

Zak swallowed hard. Her scent was in his nostrils, addling his thoughts, and he could feel the sweet outline of her body crushed against his back by her own weight. He remembered the feel of her in his arms at the dance and smothered a sigh of pure lust when she dropped her head and began to nibble on his ear. He knew their passion was borne of the desperate straights they were in, and the ever present likelihood they wouldn't survive the night, but in the heat of the moment that knowledge meant nothing to either of them.

A lithe twist, and she was in his arms, her mouth open against his own and the sweet curve of one peaking breast nestled in his palm. Despite the dangers all around them, for that instant nothing else mattered, only the straining passion of, and for, the girl he was embracing. Then a shot whined overhead and tore splinters off a nearby boulder, and they leapt apart, brought back to earth by the unexpected assault.

'They've got a man on the cliffs up by the canyon,' Zak told the girl unnecessarily. He caught hold of her and eased her up against him in the lee of one of the bigger rocks. 'He's probably as high as he can climb. If so, then we're safe enough here.'

He eyed the sun, still high in the sky, apprehensively. As the girl said, they still had a couple of hours to wait. It would be a nervy wait too, never knowing if the marksman could edge up high enough to target them again.

★ ★ ★

Once the sun sank behind the distant mountains, the darkness engulfed them quickly and Zak shifted his position to track the extending shadows.

The pair had spent most of the intervening afternoon snuggled up together, exchanging promises and confidences in tones too low to carry to the surrounding outlaws. Every so often they'd been interrupted by an isolated shot, which Zak occasionally returned to convince their enemies they were still too wide awake to be rushed.

'We'll split up,' he decided in a whisper.

'No,' Sarah Jo objected immediately, somehow aware he'd sacrifice himself to gain her an advantage if it became necessary. 'I'd sooner give myself up.'

'We'll do it my way.' Zak was unimpressed by her arguments and there was an air of finality in the tone of his voice that overawed the girl for once. 'You'll wade out into deeper water and make your way to shore further up the valley. Head for the outlaws' own township. That's the last place they'll expect to find you.' He paused to consider his own moves. 'I'll slip out the other way and meet you above the waterfall if all goes well. Don't wait there too long. If I'm more than a few minutes behind, I won't be coming.'

'You'll take them on, won't you?' If Zak could have seen in the dark, he'd have observed the tears in her eyes.

'If it's necessary.' He kept his answer short and hefted the pistol. The outlaws had them surrounded, and he knew neither of them would escape unless he provided a diversion.

Sarah Jo's soft curves unexpectedly melded against his own body when she kissed him hard, and then, just as suddenly, she was gone, obediently following his instructions. He could hear her wading into deeper water and knew the time had come.

His own entry into the lake was slow and easy. He'd taken off on the far side of the islet, thigh deep and allowed his legs to flow silently through the water until he judged he'd travelled far enough to surprise their enemies. Then he burst through the shallows firing his pistol with reckless abandon.

A thin, cut-off wail of pain was swiftly followed by a volley of return shots, so close he could almost touch the threatening barrels. The outlaws had evidently been in the process of launching their own attack under the cover of darkness, and he ducked instinctively, then surged forward again. Throwing caution to the winds, he headed for the thickest of his enemies, and in the heat of battle, with the adrenaline flowing freely, he could almost feel he had the advantage, despite the outlaws' superior fire power. He could fire indiscriminately, while their own guns were constrained by the knowledge they had to identify their target before they pulled the trigger.

His gun was emptied in no time, but Zak still surged on, cannoning into the solid bulk of first one, and then another, of the men who surrounded him, clearing a space by bludgeoning them with the pistol in his hand. One of his opponents was down and he stumbled over his body, cursing fluently while he tried to keep his balance. Another had a hold on his leg and he fell heavily, losing his grip on the pistol, but retaining enough of his senses to strike out at the man who held him.

Everyone around was shouting, a cacophony of noise, accompanied by the occasion burst of gunfire.

'Don't hurt the girl!' The Preacher's gravel voice rose above the general din and Zak felt the bitterness of defeat. Had they spotted Sarah Jo in the mêlée?

He dragged himself to his knees by main force; one man had a sinewy grip on his throat throttling him, while another hung on to his shirt. He fought on with the strength of desperation, but they were holding him down, and he saw the pistol arcing towards him before it thudded into him. The pain of the impact was like an explosion in his head, and a black vortex whirled around his brain, tunnelling his vision and slowing his thoughts.

He slumped back, barely conscious, and the fight over. Some of the outlaws were lighting torches, the dancing flames spluttering and throwing weird, demonic shadows over the surreal scene.

'Get him up here.' Zak's swirling senses recovered far enough to recognize the Preacher's voice, but his legs refused to respond when he was urged forward, and two of the outlaws had to drag him bodily on to dry land.

The Preacher stood over him and snarled angrily, lashing his face with an open hand.

'Where is she?'

Zak refused to answer, indeed was hardly capable of that much effort, and the outlaw chief hit him again.

'There's no escape for the likes of her,' he told the rancher bleakly, his eyes blazing in the spectral light of the torches. 'I mean to have her, whatever it takes.' He raised his hand threateningly again and asked the question. 'Where is she?'

'Gone.' Zak staggered to his feet to make the answer, though his brain was throbbing and his legs shook like jelly.

The Preacher hit him again, this time with his fist clenched and the rancher dropped to his knees, down again but not quite out.

'Where's the girl?' The outlaw was asking the question of his henchmen now, not the slumped form in front of him, but there was no answer forthcoming and he cursed obscenely.

Then, while the Preacher stared out into the darkness with a black look on his face, Zak breathed a sigh of relief. Sarah Jo had escaped her fate, and with any luck, she'd be on her way down the bluffs before the outlaws realized she knew the secret of the back entrance. If indeed, any of them remembered it.

'Bring him with us.' The Preacher wasted no more time in useless recrimination, and promptly stumped off towards the main township. Zak staggered forward in his wake on shaky legs, urged on by the threatening pistols of a couple of outlaws who'd been detailed to guard him.

There was an open patch behind the buildings, ironically no more than a few hundred yards from the point Zak had appointed for a rendezvous with Sarah Jo, should either of them make it that far. To his surprise he wasn't subject to any further interrogation, but allowed to sit cross legged under close guard, while he recovered his senses. Several members of the outlaw band cast him hard looks, some of them carrying the reminders of their battle in the form of blood-stained bandages, while another vowed revenge for the death of his brother. An eye for an eye.

A number of them had been set to build up a fire before a gnarled and stumpy tree that guarded the route into town, and once it had been lit, it provided a perfect illumination for the scene.

At a signal from the Preacher, Zak too was drawn forward and stationed by the tree under the thickest of its boughs, which was eight or nine feet off the ground. A rope had been thrown over it with a make-shift noose tied roughly at one end. The inference was obvious, especially when the noose was fitted loosely around the rancher's neck to a chorus of jeers from the assembled outlaws.

'Sarah!' The Preacher himself stood out and roared her name. 'Give yourself up, and we'll spare him.'

He stood and stared about the plateau; evidently he had no idea where the girl might be hiding, though he must have worked out in which direction she'd escaped the islet to avoid his men. Was that why he'd chosen this particular spot to stage his play?

At a further signal from their leader, several of the men crowded closer around Zak, tightening the noose around his neck and holding him down when he began to struggle.

'Come out, Sarah. You haven't got long to make your decision. There's some here as would be glad to see him swing.' A low cheer, and a further few jeers, greeted these words. No one in that crowd would waste their sympathy on the rancher, especially those who carried the marks of battle on them.

'Hang him.' The Preacher had lost what patience he had. The girl must still be somewhere on the plateau and he would find her at his leisure.

'Wait.' Sarah Jo appeared from the very edge of the little waterfall that ran down into the hanging valley with a rifle hanging loose in her hands. 'I'm here.'

13

Sarah Jo

Sarah Jo stepped dejectedly towards the outlaw band, still holding her rifle at the trail, while they stood staring open mouthed at her sudden appearance.

The Preacher was the first to recover his wits.

'Drop the rifle,' he commanded peremptorily.

'Let him go first.' Sarah Jo caught her weapon up in both hands, ready to use it, and the outlaw chief made an impatient sign to the men holding Zak down.

One of them loosened the noose and began to draw it over his head, while the Preacher started forward towards the girl.

'Drop the gun,' he told her again, and this time Sarah Jo did as she was bid, her head held proudly while she stared fearlessly at the oncoming outlaw.

'String him up.' The Preacher made his first mistake when he turned to issue the callous command before he was within touching distance of the girl.

With an angry start, she bent lithely, scooped up the gun and opened up a ragged fire on the motley crew that surrounded the rancher, not bothering to aim, but firing indiscriminately from the hip.

Zak kept his head, and when his captors dived for cover, flung off the noose and raced for the safety of the darkness beyond the range of the fire. Whether the suddenness of his escape, or fear of Sarah Jo's haphazard scattering of shot slowed his captors' response, he couldn't tell. He only knew he was running free in the dark without a mark on him, or even, so far as he could tell, a single shot fired at him.

Sarah Jo was still bathed in the light of the fire, and when he looked back the

Preacher held her fast in his grip. Had she run out of shells? Or simply been caught by the outlaw chief? Zak would have to re-arm before he sought out the answer to that question.

'I have the girl.' The Preacher's voice rang out loud in the night, but the rancher ignored him. That was a trick that wouldn't work twice, shouldn't even have worked once.

'She'll have an honourable marriage if you give yourself up.' The outlaw chief was playing the scene for all it was worth. 'If not, I'll take her tonight and throw her to the rest tomorrow.'

Zak doubted that; marriage to the Preacher would be anything but honourable, and the outlaw would never voluntarily sacrifice what he'd won, even to his own cohorts. If anything were clear, it was that the man desired Sarah Jo, and would have her come what may. He ran on, heading for the sheltering buildings in the outlaw's own town, the last place they'd expect to find him.

★ ★ ★

Deep in the shadows of the saloon that stood in the very centre of the outlaw's township, Zak paused to take stock of the situation. Though his head still ached unmercifully, he was otherwise recovered, but once again left without a gun of any sort to defend himself with. The Preacher and his captive had disappeared, but he could see the torches of other outlaws flickering in the darkness. Proof, if proof were needed, that he was still being hunted down. There'd be other outlaws in the little township too, he reasoned.

Guarding the girl? Not if the Preacher intended to have his way with her. More probably guarding the approaches then, and some, at least, he could hear laughing over a drink in the bar, no more than the thickness of a plank of timber away. Was that where the Preacher had his lair? Where he held Sarah Jo?

The rancher growled deep in his

throat and began to scan the length of the building, eagerly searching for an unguarded entry. An open window beckoned him forward, and he peeked cautiously over the sill into an empty room, containing a rough-hewn bed, covered with a bright coverlet and strewn untidily with clothes, women's clothes. He flung one leg over, wriggled lithely through the aperture and slipped inside, ignoring the cheap and gaudy decorations, while he flitted silently across the floor.

The door opened before he reached it and a girl entered, the same doe-eyed whore he'd marked when he first climbed into the valley. She didn't notice him at first, all her attention centred on someone, or something, in the corridor outside. Some sort of whispered flirtation seemed to be going on, but a low giggle eventually heralded her entry into the room.

Zak used one hand to stifle her mouth while his other showed her the knife. She stilled fearfully, her eyes wide with fear, while he used his foot to shut the door quietly behind them.

'Don't call out,' he warned her. 'Not if you want to live,' and dragged her across to the bed before he released her. Her eyes may have reflected her fright, but there was a knowing look in them too. The girl had evidently decided the rancher would only hurt her as a last recourse, and promptly resorted to the tools of her trade.

She was prettiest little whore in town, wasn't she? All the men told her so. A slip of the shoulder and the gaudy dress, which was all she appeared to be wearing, slid down her arm, leaving one shoulder delightfully bare. She shifted her torso in a delicate shimmy, and her bosom, the slopes of which were already bared by her low cut décolletage, trembled on the edge of complete exposure. A slow spark of hope grew in her eyes, an emotion the rancher knew he had to stifle if he wished to succeed in making her talk.

He promptly clapped his hand over

her mouth again and cuffed her hard, knocking her back on to the bed. His knife hovered over her face threatening to slice it open, but it was his eyes that convinced her. Just to imagine Sarah Jo trembling helplessly under the hands of the Preacher, as this girl trembled under his, had lit his face with an unholy light and turned his stare to flint. She shivered beneath his touch, and would have crossed herself if she'd dared to move.

'Where is she?' His hand released her mouth, and he refined the question. 'Where is Sarah Jo?'

'Down the corridor.' The knife moved down to her throat and gently pricked her skin.

'Around the corner,' she gabbled, frightened almost out of her wits by this open reminder of the power of life and death he held over her. 'It's the second door on the left. The Preacher took her there himself.'

'How long?'

'A few minutes only.' The knife drew

a slow line down her throat, its steel cold against her skin and she continued her confession. 'It's true,' she pleaded. 'I know because he's only just set a guard, standing by the corner. I spoke to him a moment ago.'

Zak remembered the girl's flirtatious behaviour before she entered the room and nodded.

'Call the guard in,' he told her.

Her eyes opened wide and she shook her head, then moaned in fear when the knife dipped again, its point hard against her throat.

'He won't come,' she explained, 'no one disobeys the Preacher, not if they want to live.' Then squealed when she felt his knife hand tense as though to drive it into her flesh. 'Please no,' she whined in absolute desperation. 'I don't like him doing this any more than you do. Aaron was my man until he saw the girl. Now he only wants her. I'll do whatever you want.'

'Then you'll help me?' The rancher regarded her suspiciously. Not that she had any choice in the matter, though what she'd do once the guard had been summoned might prove to be a horse of an entirely different colour.

'I'll help you,' she told him warily, with her eyes still fixed on the knife in his hands. 'If the guard will come to me.'

'He'll come to you,' the rancher promised her roughly, yanking her dress down until one taut breast sprang out. 'Do anything to warn him, and I promise you'll die slowly, whatever it takes.' Zak hauled the frightened girl off the bed and motioned her forward, keeping a tight grip on her arm until she opened the door. And once there, he slipped behind its concealing bulk.

'Don't try to leave the room,' he warned her in a sibilant whisper, though he could see in her eyes that survival was all she cared for at this moment.

'Ben,' she hissed, leaning forward so the man could plainly see her displaced costume. 'I'm lonely, and so are you.

Come and wait in my room.'

The guard returned an answer, but in a voice too low for Zak to hear. It was evidently an excuse the girl could override.

'I'm no longer his woman,' she replied. 'He only wants the new girl. He's besotted with her. God knows why, she's not so pretty and she doesn't love him.'

Ben was evidently still uncertain, but with a frightened glance at the rancher's set face, the girl allowed the bosom of her dress to drop completely, baring herself to the waist.

'Please,' she tried again, 'it'll be fun, and you can always go back to your duties later.'

It was a clincher and Zak measured the guard's progress by the sounds his boots made on the plain wood floor. The girl still waited on the threshold, but she was in easy reach of his knife, and she knew how vulnerable she was. She extended her arm and drew the man in, while the rancher slunk deeper into the shadows behind the door.

He would have struck there and then, probably should have, but it may have set up the sort of furore he wanted to avoid and warned the Preacher he was in the building. The girl was still enticing the guard towards her bed; the man's back was turned and he wasn't concentrating on anything but the half-naked houri beckoning him forward. Zak took the chance and slipped out of the door. If the girl wanted the Preacher to herself then it was in her interests to play along with him, allow him to steal Sarah Jo away.

He'd barely reached the corner when he realized he'd made a mistake. The girl was screeching out loud as though she was in the throes of a convulsion, and he could only hope her chaotic explanations were too incoherent for Ben to respond immediately. Next moment his target was in sight and he launched himself through the door into a room lit by the light of an oil lamp.

The Preacher had a woman pinned

down on the bed, but he'd evidently heard the commotion outside and held himself ready for anything. Zak went for him with the knife in his hand, but the outlaw dropped off the bed and scrabbled for his gun-belt, neatly coiled on a table at the bedside.

It was going to be a close run thing until Sarah Jo took a hand. Acting as calmly as though she'd rehearsed the scene, she picked up the heavy oil lamp that illuminated the room and slammed it down on the outlaw's head.

'We've got to get out.' Zak didn't slow his precipitate rush across the room one iota. He could already hear the rush of heavy boots in the corridor outside and taking the girl's hand, he urged her towards the window.

'My boots,' she shrieked, and grabbed at a pair standing neatly by a chair in the corner, before she slipped through the narrow aperture and scampered into the darkness by his side.

14

Last Stand

'Damn, you need more than boots.' Zak surveyed the girl under the light of the newly risen moon. She was engaged on drawing the footwear over her shapely feet, but it wasn't those the rancher was staring at.

Sarah Jo was wearing no more than her underwear; white bloomers that were laced in just above her knees and a thin chemise that had been torn down at the front to show more than a hint of cleavage. Both garments were finished with a froth of lace and several delicately sewn pink ribbons.

'I'm lucky to have this much clothing remaining,' she grinned at him. The pair of them may still have been in danger, but at least they were together again, and she drew her strength from that fact, silently vowing they'd die together too, rather than surrender to the outlaw's lustful vengeance.

'The women stripped off my dress and petticoats before they laid me on the bed, but it was the Preacher himself did this.' She held out her ruined neckline for his inspection. 'If you'd interrupted a minute or two later, I might have escaped with nothing left to cover my embarrassment.'

Zak ignored the fact that she didn't look in the least embarrassed, and surveyed the scene around them. They'd put several hundred yards between themselves and the township, racing across the plateau along the shores of the lake to avoid going too close to the still smouldering remains of the fire. To his dismay, most of the outlaws with torches still seemed to have congregated in that vicinity, cutting off their escape into the hanging valley. They didn't seem to have attracted any immediate form of pur-suit, probably due to the Preacher being unconscious, or maybe a general disinclination to hunt down a desperate pair of fugitives in the dark.

'Those garments are much too pale,' he told her shortly. 'They can easily be seen in the dark.'

'Shall I take them off?' the girl offered doubtfully. Then blushed when she decided she wouldn't have hesitated to do just that if Zak and her were alone on the bluffs.

'Mud,' he decided and led her down to the foreshore where there was plenty of the sticky substance to play with.

'Like this?' she questioned him, daintily speckling her underclothes with the tips of her fingers.

The rancher grunted and picked up a double handful, smearing it over her back.

'Oh!' Sarah Jo danced about shivering when the cold and wet seeped through the delicate garment. Then steeled herself to scrape up a handful herself.

'You'll have to do my bottom,' she

warned him and continued to apply the mud to the front of her costume, swallowing hard when she felt his hands on her buttocks. He was very thorough!

'This way.' Zak ran forward in fits and starts, keeping his body low, once Sarah Jo's camouflage was complete to his satisfaction. He sunk to the ground to check the disposition of their enemies at the end of every stage, while he tried to ignore the svelte lines of the figure scooting across the plateau on his heels. It was only when she was outlined against the rapidly lightening sky that he realized just how closely the wet material clung to her trim shape.

'That's where I was held,' Sarah Jo commented when they reached the adobe hut.

'Unoccupied I hope,' agreed Zak.

He sat back and stared at the building for long minutes, before he decided he had to take the chance before the rising dawn betrayed them both. He ran forward and leapt lithely towards the roof before the startled girl realized what he was about, caught hold of an edge and drew himself up. His guns were still laying where he left them and he strapped on his pistol in its holster before returning to Sarah Jo and passing her the rifle.

'There's only one way out of here for us,' he told her. 'Straight down the same path I came up.' His voice turned gruff, echoing his fears for her safety. 'We've got to be off the bluffs before first light hits us, or we're gonners. If we're separated, don't wait for me, not even for a moment.'

He caught hold of her hand and began to run towards the promise of safety, bending low to present as small a target as possible. Dawn hadn't yet broken, but reflections of its far off light had already illuminated the sky, and they were in constant danger of being silhouetted against its pale background.

A shot and the game was on, their hunters recalled from the four corners of the valley. Another shot, its passage marked by a whine close over their heads, and then they were over the cliffs, skidding down the steep, overgrown path beside the waterfall. They crashed through the undergrowth and ran along the edge of the waterhole, then drew up in dismay.

Three of the outlaws had beaten them to the hidden pathway down the bluffs. They were standing by the edge of the cliffs, but turned to stare at the newcomers, obviously as startled as the fugitives. Zak reacted first; his pistol leapt into his hand and exploded, and in the same moment he hauled Sarah Jo on to a new course.

The old guard hut, if that were its purpose, was hardly suited to defence in its current state, but it was better than nothing. It had been sited to defend against men coming over the cliff and its one and only window faced that way. Not that it mattered. Only one complete wall remained standing, and that was built into the overhang of a cliff behind, where a section of the roof still hung precariously from its rotting rafters. The remaining side was a jumble of rubble which Zak instantly tried to rearrange into a barricade high enough to protect them.

There were men coming down the cliffs on their heels to reinforce the outlaws already there, but they seemed curiously disinclined to force the pace of the conflict. Zak's pistol kept their heads down, for in the close confines of the hanging valley, it was almost impossible to withdraw beyond his range and still be in a position to train their rifles on the ruined hut.

Sarah Jo wanted to join in too, but she knew as well as the rancher, that she had only the shells remaining in its breech to fire. She'd keep them to beat back the assault that would surely come.

The Preacher was there too, far back by the waterfall, out of their sight, but not out of mind, for his voice carried on the wind.

It was a stalemate, or so Zak began to think. They were under cover, if not exactly safe in the ruin, and the outlaws plainly didn't want to rush the building under fire from two well armed and desperate fugitives. They may even have defied their formidable boss if he'd ordered it; the Preacher himself!

Not that it mattered to the defenders in the long run. They had no access to water; sooner or later they'd succumb to the demon thirst and become too weak to defend themselves. Before it came to that, he swore, he'd foray out himself and sell his life dearly.

Sarah Jo had evidently thought through the options too. 'We'll hit them as soon as the sun sets,' she told him simply, too exhausted by the constant threats to be afraid.

Zak slipped his arm around her shoulders and she relaxed trustingly against him.

The Preacher wasn't so patient, however, and he had an unexpected ace up his sleeve. Dynamite. His explosive expert was laying in a bed back at the township, his leg a useless mass of broken bones where a shell had smashed it on the edge of the lake, but how difficult could it be? He bound four sticks together and detailed a man to light the fuse and run forward to toss it close to the ruins. Not so close it would harm the girl, but close enough for the outlaws to advance under cover of the debris loosened by its blast.

Zak almost missed the outlaw when he charged into the open. The move was not only unexpected, but suicidal, and so it proved when the rancher picked him off with a single, well aimed shot. The man staggered and fell, but managed to toss the multiple sticks of dynamite forward before he died.

It should have ended up closer to the ruin than it did, and both sides watched the fuse burn down with grim, if fearful, fascination. Zak drew Sarah Jo down to the floor in the far corner of the ruin and covered her with his body; the outlaws lay low and covered their heads as best they could. The dynamite went off in a shattering explosion, and for long moments neither side could do any more than attempt to regain their shattered senses.

This was the moment for the Preacher's reserve, deliberately held back by the waterfall out of harm's way, to make their move. Instead they suddenly came under fire from above.

It wasn't apparent to Zak at first that the outlaws were fighting on two fronts. The wall they'd been sheltering behind had blown in and he was covered by debris from the explosion and the choking miasma of dust that blinded him to anything happening more than a foot or two away. What remained of the roof had fallen in too, a huge slab of it arched at a crazy angle over their heads, only the remnants of the corner they'd chosen as shelter holding its bulk in check.

Sarah Jo was alive, he could feel her body wriggling under his own, trying to free herself no doubt, though it didn't occur to his shattered brain to move. He could hear the shooting had redoubled in its intensity too, but it took some time for its import to trickle through his addled mind. He felt around weakly for his pistol, but it was gone, and he resigned himself to defeat.

All of a sudden the mass of roof above them shifted and Sarah Jo was screaming in his ear. What did she want? He could feel her squirming past him in the confined space, and then hauling him across the rubble by his feet.

There was a further rumble and more choking dust when the last remnants of the roof finally crumbled on to the rubble strewn floor, but by that time Zak was laid on the grass outside. Sarah Jo was bathing his forehead with cool water, he could see her face above him. Where were the outlaws? Surely the Preacher should be stringing him up!

★　★　★

It was several minutes before Zak recovered his wits far enough to understand what had been occurring up on the bluffs while they were fighting a desperate rearguard action against the outlaw band in the hanging valley.

Sarah Jo was still fussing around him, once more decently dressed, in an old, badly stained blanket she'd hastily converted into a makeshift poncho to cover her scanty, and quite frankly, filthy undergarments. The federal marshal, who'd evidently listened to the sheriff's plea for help in dealing with the Ghost Riders, was there too. And it was he who offered an explanation to the puzzle, the answers to which still evaded the rancher's brain.

'It took us some time to gather the posse,' the lawman told him. 'We needed to recruit a sizeable band to force an entrance on to the bluffs, but we followed on as quickly as we could. It was nervy work under threat of the outlaws' guns, but we infiltrated the canyon in the dark last night, and coincided our attack with the dawn.

Took some casualties too, though nowhere near as many as we would have if the Preacher had stationed all his men on the entrance. Fact is, we probably shouldn't have succeeded at all in that case.

'There was no one left in the buildings up top, even the women seemed to have fled, but we could hear the gunshots coming from this direction and set off hot foot to see what was going on. There was a massive explosion just as we reached the edge of the valley which startled us as much as anyone.' He stared at the filthy, blood encrusted face in front of him and coughed politely. 'Perhaps not as much as you,' he allowed, 'but some. None of us could understand what was happening, but we could see the gang milling about below, and guessed they were up to no good.

'We knew Sarah Jo had to be about somewhere, quite possibly holed up, so we opened up on them varmints immediately. Had them caught like rats in a trap, or so we thought.' He had the grace to look a little crestfallen when he explained. 'The Preacher fought his way free, couple of the others with him. There's more than one path down here and he knew them all. I despatched some of the boys after him, but he gave them the slip. I dare say he's skedaddled clear out of the territory by now.'

'I hope so.'

Zak made a feeble attempt to stand, then sank back down again. Sheer exhaustion had combined with the concussive effects of the explosion to leave him weak as the proverbial kitten.

15

The Preacher

Zak, laid low by the aftermath of concussion, had to be carried down from the bluffs and conveyed to town in a wagon. But once in a bed in the banker's apartment, despite Sarah Jo's dismal imaginings, he quickly began to regain his strength. A healthy constitution and the assiduous attentions of his nurse contributed in equal parts to his swift recovery, and within a day or two he was sitting up demanding his clothes.

'Doc won't be able to see you until later this afternoon,' Sarah Jo told him reprovingly.

'Damn it, Sarah Jo. There's nothing wrong with me.' He eyed her with a glint in his eye. 'I'd get up and find them myself if I wasn't naked as a jaybird.'

'Go ahead,' she grinned engagingly. 'I've seen you that way before. Who do you think put you to bed? In any case, you won't find your clothes in the apartment, they're hanging on the line out back. Filthiest basket of washing I ever saw.'

'I'm surprised you do your own washing,' he said, querying her house-keeping. He knew the Mountjoys had a woman come in every day to keep things tidy.

'I don't normally,' she replied airily, 'but I'm practising for when you carry me off to our ranch.' Sarah Jo had put off all thought of leaving the territory.

'Who says I'll take you.'

'Zachariah Carter!' Sarah Jo stood with her hands on her hips and attempted an outraged expression. 'You're not going to refuse me, not when I spent an entire night alone with you up on the bluffs. My reputation would be in tatters.'

She'd overplayed her hand, and she giggled when Zak reached out a brawny arm to capture her.

'No,' she shrieked, but she didn't struggle when he pulled her down to the bed at his side. Nor did she act at all coy and attempt to stop his kisses.

'Sarah Jo!'

'Father.' The girl blushed red and wriggled out of the rancher's embrace.

'Well . . . ' The banker hadn't been happy about the pairing, but with all the rancher had done for his daughter, he'd been brought to accept that Zak was the man she'd have. Not that he intended to countenance her grappling on the bed with a naked man before the banns had been read.

'I don't think . . . ' he began again, then thought back to his own sweetheart, Sarah Jo's mother. 'I suppose it doesn't matter what I think,' he admitted. 'Just try to be a little more circumspect until you're married.'

'You didn't come just to tell us that.' Zak was staring at the banker's worried countenance.

'The Preacher,' and the man suddenly

looked old beyond his years. 'The Preacher has delivered an ultimatum to me.' He looked up, staring straight into the rancher's face. 'You know he escaped, of course. We all thought he'd leave the territory with what remained of his gang, but it seems we were wrong.'

'Where is he?' Zak's voice was measured, but there was no doubting the hatred in its inflexion.

'I don't know. The message was delivered direct to the bank and one of the tellers brought it up.'

'What did it say?'

'He wants you to meet him out on Main Street at noon today. He intends to take Sarah Jo once he's killed you.'

'No, Zak. You can't.' The girl broke in on their conversation, but she may as well have held her breath.

'I've already been to see the sheriff,' continued the banker without acknowledging her outburst. 'He's despatched a rider to the marshal's office. There'll be a federal posse in town by nightfall. We can hide you until then.'

'Hide from that mangy dog.' Zak flung back the covers regardless. 'I won't do it. Get my clothes, Sarah Jo.'

The girl didn't offer any excuses this time. She'd seen the expression on her man's face. She didn't want him to face down the formidable outlaw, but she knew when his mind was made up.

★ ★ ★

Another saloon, another gun fight, but this time Zak wasn't in the least interested in the attractions of the hostesses. He was still warm from the kisses Sarah Jo had rained on his face, the soft weight of her body in his arms, the scent of her perfume. He wasn't frightened by the outlaw chief's fearsome reputation either. Why should he be, when he'd spent a large part of his life just waiting for this confrontation. He was ready for the shooting to begin.

Man to man, this time; his enemy, and so often his nemesis. The Preacher was his to kill, and his only! He'd shoot the outlaw down this very day and rob the hangman, even if it took his last breath to do the deed.

He drank down the shot in a single gulp, one drink only to steady his nerves, and strode out on to the street. It wasn't quite noon, but he fancied the Preacher would be ready whenever he was. The town was quiet, too quiet for a busy weekday, but the rancher realized the townsfolk would be watching from whatever hiding place they'd scuttled into. The sheriff too, if he hadn't packed up altogether and gone off fishing.

All to the good, he decided. If the law was too weak to take a stand, then it would be cheated of the outlaw's capture. Vengeance on the Preacher was his own to take. A good day for it too, he decided irreverently. The sun was riding high in a clear blue sky, but the air seemed particularly clear, and the far off bluffs were in plain view, shimmering prettily in the heat.

Where the man appeared from, Zak had no idea, nor did it matter. The street had been empty until the Preacher edged out in front of him, his long, dark frock coat flung back and his right hand hovering over the deadly gun laid in its holster.

'Time to die, boy.' The Preacher's gravelled tones echoed harshly over the dusty street, but if he'd hoped to overawe the young rancher he was disappointed.

Zak hadn't even listened to what his opponent said, let alone allowed himself to be psyched out. His eyes were engaged in searching further down the street — a man of the Preacher's ilk would have backup to hand. He might have absolute confidence in his own skill with the gun, but he'd still post whatever men still clung to his banner where they could back his play.

There was one lying prone up on the flat roof of the building opposite, the long, slim barrel of a rifle pushed forward in front of him, held loose. So they weren't planning to shoot him down before the gunfight began!

Another? The dark alleyway that led towards the graveyard caught hold of Zak's imagination. Had he spotted the echo of a movement in its shadows? His eyes searched again, assessing the available cover; if he was still standing when the gunsmoke lifted, he'd have to move fast.

'The girl's mine for the taking.' The Preacher, his face as harsh as his voice, tried again, but his opponent refused to be drawn by the other's taunts.

Zak's mouth was dry and his heart began to thump. His palm was slick with sweat, but he wasn't afraid of his infamous opponent. The rancher knew exactly what he had to do, even if he had to die in attempting it.

The outlaw's eyes flickered briefly, right and left, checking his men were in position, and Zak decided the time had come. He began his draw at the same time as his opponent and they cleared leather in unison. He stood firm to fire a fraction ahead of the Preacher, then dropped prone to the ground, rolling right, where he had a horse trough to shelter under. He'd been hit in the shoulder, but he didn't know how bad — no time to find out either.

The Preacher was down too, dead or dying by the look of it, but he had no time to confirm that either. The man on top of the building was firing and the water trough offered a less than solid barrier against rifle fire from above. He tried a snap shot himself and uttered a grunt of triumph; the man showed his nerves under fire and retreated further under cover of the roof. Zak pulled the trigger again and made a run for it, firing once more to keep his opponent's head down. He slipped into a narrow alleyway, sheltering in the shadow of the buildings either side and shot again.

His shoulder hurt and his head was beginning to spin, but, summoning up all his resolution, he began to sprint, frantically reloading his gun while he ran. He was only a block below the graveyard and the alleyway that led down past the church was in his sights. There was a man posted in the shadows there; he hadn't seen him, but he was sure of his facts. If he could reach the far end of that narrow passage then he'd hold the advantage, with the outlaw silhouetted against the sun streaming in from Main Street.

In fact he didn't have to run that far. The outlaw had evidently seen where the fight was going and cut and run himself, or perhaps he was simply attempting the same trick as his opponent. Be that as it may, the man burst out of the alleyway no more than a couple of yards in front of Zak and the rancher duly shot him down.

The marksman on the roof was no longer in place by the time Zak reached Main Street again. A thunder of hoofs showed where he'd made his escape and the rancher ran out into the open to take a snap shot. Then he allowed his gun to drop; the man was well out of effective pistol range and Zak was sick of killing.

He cautiously approached the Preacher's body instead, levelling his pistol on the man, while he turned him with his boot. The outlaw was dead, and his reign of terror at an end.

* * *

The young lad lifted determined eyes up the bluffs towards two mossy horned old cows that had somehow scaled the mountainous heights. His gaze took in the perilously constricted animal paths that scarred the cliff face, no more than narrow fissures cut into the solid rock, and he began to toil up the steep ascent.

He'd left his horse far below, and he cursed his boots that were made for riding, and not for clambering up such steep slopes. He stopped for a moment, sweating heavily in the summer sun, and stared off into the distance. His keen eyes could just about make out the ranch house his ma and pa had completed the year he was born, no doubt they'd both be down there right now. Pa was constructing a new barn and his younger siblings would be helping. Zak was named for his father, and Sarah Jo for her mother, though she was such a tomboy, they may as well have named her for a boy.

He, himself, was named Tom, apparently in honour some sort of local hero who'd once stood out against a bunch of outlaws to save Pa's life. Pa had fought the outlaws too, or so he'd been told. Outfaced a gunman down on Main Street, if the reports were true. But then, they probably weren't; he'd never seen his pa with a gun-belt strapped around his hips, and nor could he ever imagine such a thing. His pa was a peaceable man!

No outlaws in town now, of course. It was the first year of a new century, and the territory had moved on since those desperate days.

We do hope that you have enjoyed reading this large print book.

Did you know that all of our titles are available for purchase?

We publish a wide range of high quality large print books including:
Romances, Mysteries, Classics
General Fiction
Non Fiction and Westerns

Special interest titles available in large print are:
The Little Oxford Dictionary
Music Book, Song Book
Hymn Book, Service Book

Also available from us courtesy of Oxford University Press:
Young Readers' Dictionary
(large print edition)
Young Readers' Thesaurus
(large print edition)

For further information or a free brochure, please contact us at:
Ulverscroft Large Print Books Ltd.,
The Green, Bradgate Road, Anstey,
Leicester, LE7 7FU, England.
Tel: (00 44) 0116 236 4325
Fax: (00 44) 0116 234 0205

OUTLAW QUEEN

Ethan Flagg

In Wyoming, an outlaw gang named the Starrbreakers causes mayhem. After every robbery the bandits vanish into the stronghold of the Big Horn Mountains through a gap known as the Hole in the Wall. The law authorities are powerless to hunt them down, so Special Agent Drew Henry is hired to infiltrate the gang in the guise of an escaped convict. Bullets will fly when he comes to town. When Henry takes on the Outlaw Queen can he break the Starrbreakers' stranglehold?

THE LONG HUNT

Alan Irwin

In Amarillo, Texas Ranger Dan Kennedy hears that his young nephew, Jamie, has been kidnapped from Dan's father's place, the Rocking K Ranch. Finding the boy has been captured by the Morgan gang, Dan vows to hunt them down and bring Jamie safely home. He heads south with expert tracker Josh Brennan, but the gang soon become aware of their pursuers, leaving Dan and Josh vulnerable to attack. Can they survive this formidable threat and bring Jamie home alive?

THE DRUMMOND BRAND

William DuRey

In Montana, settlers around the township of Bridger Butte were forced out by a ruinous winter. Their properties were bought by Luther Drummond, owner of the Diamond-D ranch, amid rumours that the settler's misfortunes were attributable to Luther's son, Dagg. Embroiled in the town's affairs, Pinkerton detective Ethan Brodie is accused of murder and stagecoach robbery. Ethan and Claire Dumbril, the victim's daughter, vow to find the killers, but how will they fare and what perils await them?

LAST RECKONING FOR THE PRESIDIO KID

Emmett Stone

A stagecoach robbery and a train explosion announce the sudden return of the elusive Presidio Kid. Little is known about the Kid, or what triggered these events. In an isolated mountain cabin, Clugh Bendix nurses a leg wound, vowing to discover who shot him. He must travel to the volatile Texas borderlands, to the heart of the mystery of the Presidio Kid. The mystery becomes a battle and he must rely on his wits and his guns to survive.